I0551673

Frozen Lies the Librarian
by Penny Johnston

Penny Johnston, Publisher

Penny Johnston, Publisher

The characters and events in this book are fictitious. Any similarity to real persons, living or dead, is coincidental and not intended by the author.

ISBN: 9780993997938

Cover Design by Sara Carrick

Detective and Mystery stories, Canadian (English). Johnston, Penny

Dedicated to The late Lillian Elliot Uren, Richard and Wendy Johnston

Acknowledgements

Thank you to Robert Barnett (cover photo), Mary Calder and Alex Wilmot, editors and cover artist Sara Carrick

Penny Johnston

Chapter 1

It was a cool, crisp day with two weeks remaining until Christmas. The sky was a chilling bright blue. The wind had died down. Lake Couchiching, frozen solid for two weeks, was safe enough now to walk out on the ice.

David Scott, a constable with the Mariposa OPP detachment decided to take a couple of hours off for a little R and R this Saturday morning. He'd drive his snowmobile along the lakeshore and maybe stop, chop a hole in the ice and do a little ice fishing.

Even though Mariposa had been his home for the past two years, David still felt like an outsider. Sure the people were friendly enough, but he was not part of the community. These things take time he told himself. This year Christmas held no joy for him.

Down by the lake, he could study the blue and grey stripes of the horizon, the harbour grey etchings of the ice and snow, the black greys of distant cottages, the green and greys of fir trees covered in snow and the children's summer camps away in the distance. At this season, grey had become his favourite colour. He hoped that the cold air would numb his brain.

Coming along the shoreline where the ice was thick, David found his favourite spot, roughly a quarter mile down the lake from Mariposa, near the channel where he knew the fish liked to hide.

Two or three strong chops with his axe and he had a hole in the ice for his line. Then he sat down on a wooden box and waited and waited. Finally, his line moved. Nice try, thought David, when he pulled up his line. But the fish had gotten away. Try again. But he hesitated. The wind was starting up. The sky overhead was turning from grey to black. Heavy snow clouds were forming. A storm was brewing. The wind blowing in off the bay, down the channel to the lake, was telling him to leave. The shadows of the fir trees had lengthened across the ice. He looked back at Mariposa and could barely make out the white gothic church spire in the grey darkness.

Hurry home, hurry home, whistled the north wind.

But just as he was speeding back to the right of a tiny island, opposite the park on shore, he saw a flash of red on the ice. He cut the snowmobile's engine and headed closer. It was a long red mohair scarf lying on the ice. Where did it come from? He stooped to pick it up. But, as his eyes followed the length of the scarf, he saw a woman almost covered by a snowdrift lying in the shadow of the ice and rock overhang of the shore.

From a distance, she looked like she was sleeping. Her waist length raven hair was fanned out around her face and shoulders. Her arms were flung out from her body like a snow angel. She lay there on her back in her brown, down coat and knee high leather boots like a China doll thrown down on the ice. He rushed over and knelt down beside her, but he knew before he touched her that she was dead.

He brushed the flakes of snow off her freckled cheeks and forehead. He recognized her. It gave him a bit of a shock. It was Cathy Snifton, the assistant librarian. He had met her several times when he had dropped off his wife's books at the library. Cathy, a pale, thin, young woman, had helped him find a book by Dr. Carl Hanson on How to Handle Stress.

Poor Cathy, she looked more beautiful dead than alive. The tension around her mouth had gone. He put his fingers to her eyelids and closed them.

Next he gently brushed away the rest of the snow from her face and her neck, with the back of his glove. In doing so, he noticed the bruise mark and the wide plum coloured band of skin, like a necklace, encircling her neck, just above her Adam's apple. Those were strangulation marks.

David went back to his snowmobile and took his cell phone from one of the rear saddle pockets. Even off duty, he always carried it with him, never knowing when immediate help was needed.

He called the office. He could hear the crackle, crackle on the line, then Clancy's voice.

"Hey, Clancy, David here. Something serious has come

up. I've found a body down by the lake."

"I thought you were off duty this morning?"

"I was until now. I found a young woman's frozen body down by the lake, along the shoreline. I think she's been strangled."

"Good grief," said Clancy, "the second murder in Mariposa in five years and you have to go and find it. I'll send Dr. Frost, the coroner, the photographer and the scene identification officers out to help you. Stand by." Another crackle on the line.

"David, why did you have to be so keen, to go out and find yourself a corpse on a Saturday morning, two weeks before Christmas when we're so short staffed? Why couldn't you have waited until after the holidays?"

"Knock it off, Clancy. A young woman has been murdered. I'll wait until you get here."

David put back the phone and then took out a notebook and began writing. "Fully clothed, female Caucasian, Height 158 cm. Weight approximately ninety kilograms. Wearing a brown Duvet coat, knee-high leather boots and red mittens. No sign of a purse or hat. Red mohair scarf found on ice beside her. Time the body was discovered, nine-thirty a.m."

He looked around, no footprints, nothing in the snow. The wind had taken care of that. This is going to be a tough one, he thought. It must be at least minus twenty degrees Celsius today. He stamped his feet to keep warm.

Geeze, he thought, it will take them a half hour to get organised and get out here.

Last year at this time, how different it had all been. He and Julia had gone out together to choose a tree at Shaw's farm. He had cut down a lovely little spruce. Together they had dragged it through the heavy snow to their car where he had lashed it to the roof. Then they'd driven home to their cosy little apartment. He had built a fire with logs in the fireplace, while Julia had made hot chocolate and popcorn. Together they had strung up the lights and strung the branches with strings of popcorn while listening to Christmas music on the local FM station.

There was no tree this year. No decorations. His

apartment was bleak and barren. He hated to return to it at the end of the day. He reached up and wiped the build-up of moisture on his goggles.

Christmas was only two weeks away and he couldn't face it. He couldn't stand those cheerful faces in the streets peering into windows, shopping for gifts for loved ones. He hated overhearing his colleagues in the office planning their holidays—holidays in the sun—visiting relatives, planning the Christmas dinner.

Julia is dead, he wanted to scream at them. Julia is dead. Keep busy, he told himself and you won't have time to think. But no matter how hard he worked at forgetting, he couldn't blot out the pain. His wife of one year was dead.

Now he was standing alone on a bleak, cold Saturday morning with the cold eating at every bone in his body, beside the body of another young woman.

When would they get here?

Thankfully in the distance he could hear the snapping of branches, the clomping of boots breaking through the surface of ice and snow.

"Where the hell are you, David? We need a search party to find you?"

He recognized Clancy's voice.

"Over here. I'm over here in the clearing."

Jovial, Clancy, 130 kilograms of him, with a pot belly that reminded David of Santa Claus, stumbled through the deep snow, puffing and wheezing, leading the group into the clearing.

"David," said Clancy, "We finally found you! Bob White, Scene Identification Officer, will be in charge of the investigation. The Barrie office loaned him to us."

Oh no, thought David, a real snotty shit is brought in from Barrie, as if we couldn't handle this ourselves. He bit his lip. "She's over there."

Dr. Jerry Frost, the county coroner, bundled up against the strong winds in a raccoon coat, went immediately over to the body.

"How long has she been dead, doc?"

"I can give you an approximate time, but the most

8

accurate time will be determined by the autopsy," said Dr. Frost cautiously. "There's frostbite on her face, her nose and her fingers. But her internal organs are still warm. Her core temperature is twenty-six degrees centigrade. To give you an idea, when an adult dies, the body cools at a rate of one degree per hour. Based on this, I would give an approximate time of between ten or twelve hours previously. A rough guess would be that she was killed between eleven and three o'clock last night."

"Any idea of how she was killed?" asked White with a superior air.

"It looks like she was strangled." Dr. Frost pointed to the wide plum band encircling her neck with bruises above and below the band. With tweezers, he bent over to pluck up something. "Here's something for your collection, White." He held up a red wool fibre. "This was imbedded in the skin of her neck. Her clothes and her underwear will be tested for fibres, debris and blood stains at the Centre for Forensic Science. A laser there will pick up any fingerprints found on the body."

"Do you think that she was killed here?"

"Maybe, I can't tell for sure until I check for signs of lividity on the body. She may have been killed elsewhere and dumped here."

"Mm," mused White, "this is a pretty remote place for anyone to come, especially a woman on their own late at night. Why would she come out this far on the lake? If she did come. One more question, doc, was the victim sexually assaulted?"

"In my opinion, just briefly glancing at the body and checking that her underwear is intact. I would say no. Her underwear has not been disturbed. The lab will do a test for semen, pubic hairs, and stains on the underwear just in case." Dr. Frost closed his bag and got to his feet.

"Thank you, doc. Can you find your way back to your car? When will the autopsy report be ready?"

"I could have it ready by Tuesday at the earliest. The Centre tests will take longer."

"That's fine by me. It will give us something to start on." White turned to the rest of the group. "Gentlemen," he commanded, "we've got our work cut out for us. Let's look for broken branches, fibres, objects dropped in the snow, anything at all that can be tied to this killing and to the direction the killer came from."

"Clancy, get out the yellow tape and mark off the area." White turned to David, "You're the one that found the body, right? You and I will begin sifting the snow. Before we begin we can take casts of any footprints, in the snow. A bit tricky, but we can do it. Did you notice any?"

"None," replied David, "except mine. The wind and the drifting snow have wiped out all the footprints that were there. Besides there is a snow base of only a couple of inches, beneath that is all ice."

For half an hour, David and White worked quietly on the boring task of sifting through the snow. But their search didn't show up anything.

"Nothing, absolutely nothing," said White discouraged. "We'll make sure there are enough photographs of the body, the location and the relationship of the body to the shore. Then we will call it a day."

White paused, then turned to David, "I'm putting you in charge of the investigation for the next couple of days. I can't because I am working on two other homicides in Barrie. You don't have any pressing family needs, do you?"

David winced, "No, not anymore." He thought, the bastard unloading the investigation off on me in the dead of winter.

White, seeing the tense look on David's face, said, "Don't worry, David, the rest of the guys will give you back-up. You won't be totally on your own. Think of it as a challenge. It is just for a few days."

Yeah, sure, thought David. That's what they all say when they want you to do something nasty. He sighed. Yes, he would do it. His free time that morning had already been shot to hell.

*****

David hated what he had to do next, tell the next of kin. It was his job, thanks to White, and it had to be done. He had to tell a mother that her daughter was dead. He was only doing his duty, but this was the most unpleasant part of it all. A corpse was one thing, but coping with grief from the living was even worse.

He remembered how he felt when the doctor, still in his operating gown, had come out of the operating room and stood silently in front of him.

"Your wife is dead," the doctor had simply said. "There were complications. Your wife suffered from a brain embolism. It was nothing we could have foreseen. Nothing we could control. We have done our best. I'm terribly sorry to tell you this."

David had felt a sudden stab at the heart. Then there was no feeling at all. Nothing. The doctor had to be lying. In childbirth? Since when did a mother die in childbirth? Not since the Middle Ages. But not now! God, not now in the twenty-first century!

Aloud he cursed Julia. How could she have left him to this emptiness? He must get control of his emotions. He kicked himself and inhaled the cold air. His breath came out in little white clouds in front of him as he approached Cathy's home.

He opened the Victorian iron grill gate and tramped up the long icy path to the house. There were no fresh footprints in the snow. No footprints at all. His were the first on the path. The Snifton home, an old three-storey Victorian house with gingerbread trim and gables needed a fresh coat of paint. He noticed the missing spindles in the veranda railing and how melting ice had dripped through a broken eavestrough. The house looked neglected and uncared for. He found the bell by the side of the door and pushed it.

He heard the shuffling of slippered feet and the tapping of a cane along the hardwood floor. To the side of the door, a white lace curtain was drawn back and a grey haired woman looked out at him, curiously. She shook her head from side to side and mouthed, I don't want anything.

David held his I.D. up against the window pane, so that she could read it.

She pursed her lips. Then the lace curtain fell back into

place and he could hear her shuffle to the front door and slowly unlock it.

"Mrs. Snifton, I'm from Mariposa OPP. I have bad news. Your daughter..." he thought, I can't tell her out in the cold standing here on the veranda.

"My daughter?" she asked with a worried look.

"Yes, may I come in Mrs. Snifton?"

He followed her shuffling steps into the darkened front living room. She fumbled along the wall until she found the light switch.

David glanced around the large room. Hand-painted china plates of roses and chrysanthemums delicately sketched on china rested on a ledge which ran around the circumference. A Royal Doulton figure of the Good Shepherd stood on top of the TV set. On the floor lay a worn Persian rug. He could see cracker crumbs and bits of hair, probably the cat's, on its pile surface. The red velvet Victorian Empire sofa, to one side of the room looked too delicate to sit on. He chose to stand. "Your daughter," he coughed to get her attention.

But Mrs. Snifton interrupted. "You want to see her? I haven't seen Cathy this morning. She must have slept in. She never bothers me Saturday morning. She must still be up in her bedroom," said Mrs. Snifton slumping down in an over-stuffed chair in front of the TV set. A pile of newspapers and a tray of dirty dishes sat on a little coffee table next to her. She plucked nervously at the cloth on the arm rest.

"Mrs. Snifton," he said softly, "your daughter is dead."

"She can't be. You have the wrong person. Cathy's sleeping upstairs. She's just slept in. Come. I'll show you. We'll go up together."

In the hall she grabbed the banister and eased herself slowly up the stairs, one foot at a time. David followed her. She turned to him at the top.

"Cathy's room was once my sewing room, when I was first married," said Mrs. Snifton with a wistful glance. "I have my bedroom next to the bathroom in case I have to get up during the night."

She banged on the door with her cane.

"Cathy, it's me, your mother. Cathy," demanded Mrs.

Snifton, her voice rising, "I have something important I want to discuss with you."

They waited. There was only the sound of the north wind pressing against the window pane. and the creaking of the floor boards. Frantically, Mrs. Snifton stumbled against the door and pushed it open. Cathy's large, white, iron, four poster bed, with the white lace bedspread, two heart shaped pillows and a Teddy Bear, was empty. The bed hadn't been slept in. Mrs. Snifton threw herself down on the bed wailing, "Cathy, Cathy, my beautiful daughter. What has happened to you?"

"Cathy is dead," said David simply.

"Cathy dead? You're lying. She can't be."

David wondered just when the reality of the horror which had happened to this woman's daughter would sink in. How long would it take?

"Are you sure, it's her and not someone else?"

"I want you to come with me, and identify Cathy's body."

"Cathy, Cathy," howled Mrs. Snifton, her tear stained face buried in a pillow. "What will I do without you? How will I manage?"

David looked around the room, at the faded rosebud wallpaper, the white lace curtains on brass rings. On the wall were prints by Monet, painted in his garden at Giverny, France. He remembered how Julia had loved the water lilies. "We'll go there some day, just you and I," he'd said. Julia had laughed, "That's a promise."

Mrs. Snifton followed his gaze. "Cathy fixed it up herself. I can't do much because of my arthritis."

"Excuse me, while I look at her things."

David walked over to the closet and opened the door. Inside he recognized the tiny flower patterns of Laura Ashley wool dresses with their white lacy collars. His wife had one. Expensive. He looked down at the shoes. Several pairs of flats and one pair of heels were lined up neatly in a row.

He looked over at the bookcase. Jane Austen's *Pride and Prejudice, Wuthering Heights, Jane Eyre, Middlemarch, Vanity Fair*, all classics. Nothing unusual here.

"Did she keep a diary, Mrs. Snifton?"

"None that I know of."

He crossed over to the dresser and looked at the pieces of jewellery in a silver tray on the bureau. There was a cameo pin in an antique gold frame. It looked expensive.

"That was my mother's. I gave it to Cathy when she turned eighteen."

David dropped the single strand of pearls into his hand. It looked good. So did the pearl stud earrings and the tiny filigree gold chain. He wondered who had given them to her. A little figure on silver skates poised ready to twirl on a patch of silver paper atop a wooden music box caught his eye. David smiled. He opened the lid to look inside. As he did so, he activated the box. He recognized the tune, '*The Skater's Waltz*'. There was nothing inside and he shut the lid down again quickly. This was not the time to be frivolous.

To the side of the music box, in a small porcelain dish, were several lipsticks, a comb and a brush and a small compact.

Mrs. Snifton pursed her lips. "She didn't use much makeup."

"Did she take any medication?"

"None that I know of."

"Was she on the pill, Mrs. Snifton?"

"She never told me, if she was. Cathy was a good girl," sniffed Mrs. Snifton into her hanky. "She never gave me any trouble."

David walked over to the dresser drawer, "May I?"

He felt that he was violating the dead girl's personal space as he pulled open the top drawer of her dresser and knelt down feeling for something hidden or shoved to the rear of the drawer. He was looking for a diary. The first drawer held a jumble of pantyhose. The second drawer contained her lingerie. He felt his face redden as he pulled out a jumble of black lacy garter belts.

"Nothing here," he mumbled. The bottom drawer held other under garments—a tangle of light and frothy black bikini pants and bras—the kind that Lovecraft sold.

Mrs. Snifton looked puzzled. "I wasn't aware..." she

began, her voice trailing off.

"What kind of girl was Cathy?" asked David softly. "Who were your daughter's friends? Tell me what you know."

Mrs. Snifton sobbed nervously. "She never brought anyone home. My daughter was a quiet, sensitive girl. She kept her thoughts to herself. She had two good friends, Clara Clarke and James Muir. But I never saw them.

"I don't know what I am going to do without her. She was always so helpful to me. I have severe rheumatoid arthritis. My joints are swollen. At times I can hardly walk. I take aspirin and cortisone, but sometimes it isn't enough. I need Cathy. I need my daughter. What will I do? Without her, I am helpless. I am lost."

Mrs. Snifton closed her eyes. She rocked back and forth, back and forth on the edge of the bed.

"I can hardly get through a day without pain. I spend my time reading paperbacks, the newspapers, the books that Cathy brings back from the library. Then at the end of the day, I watch at the window for her to come home and get supper. For lunch I just have a sandwich and a cup of soup that Cathy has left in the refrigerator for me."

"Did Cathy seem upset lately?"

"The only thing I noticed was that she had lost her appetite. She always loved her food. No matter how much she ate she never put on a pound. I thought that she was worried about something at work." Mrs. Snifton's voice broke. "If only she had said something. But I didn't ask her and she never said anything."

"Did anyone call her on the telephone? Did she get many phone calls in the evening?"

"When the phone rang, I didn't answer it. I'm usually watching television. Cathy doesn't want to bother me, so when it rings, she picks up the phone on the extension in the hall."

"Did you ever answer the phone in the evening when she wasn't here? Do you recall anyone calling for Cathy? Do you recall any man asking for your daughter?"

Mrs. Snifton pursed her lips. "James, a boy that she went out with occasionally, was one person who called. He's a bit of a momma's boy. He wouldn't harm a fly. So polite, you might as well put an apron on him."

"Did Cathy have a special boyfriend? Did she go out with anyone?"

"I don't think so. She never mentioned anyone in particular to me. She went out with James."

"Had she seen him lately?"

"Never mentioned it to me."

"Did your daughter have any close friends? Anyone whom she could confide in?"

"As I said, she never brought anyone home. But she sometimes met for coffee, with some of her old school friends. She had one close friend, Clara, who sang in the church choir. They would go to movies together and concerts sometimes." She nodded, "Talk to Clara Clarke."

"Where does Clara Clarke live?"

"Below the hill. She inherited a cottage after her parents died. On Brant Street, I believe."

David wrote down the address in his notebook.

"Did Cathy bring Clara home?"

"No, why should she? There's nothing for her here," said Mrs. Snifton sharply. "I can't entertain anyone in my condition."

It was Cathy's home too, thought David. It was Cathy's money and energy that was keeping this place going, obviously a thankless task.

"So nobody came to the house?"

"No, I never saw anyone."

"Can you tell me about her hobbies? Her interests?"

"She liked the outdoors. She liked to skate down at that rink by the lake. She liked the exercise. I thought it was a good idea for her to get some colour in her cheeks. It's supervised, you know."

Then Mrs. Snifton realized the irony of her words. She broke down sobbing. "Was it... was it near there that they found the body?"

David didn't answer. Instead he said, "Do you have a good friend? Someone who can come over after you have identified Cathy?"

"Mrs. Sandy, the doctor's wife, is always so kind. I don't

know her well. I don't know if she will come."

"I'll call her. Maybe she can fix you up with a nice cup of tea."

He would come back to ask her more questions when she was feeling better.

His next stop would be the library where Cathy worked. An interview with the formidable Mrs. Proudfoot was something he didn't relish at all. Not at all.

*****

Mariposa Memorial Library stood on Main Street near a little park adjacent to the opera house. The library had been built at the turn of the century, like many small town libraries, with funds from the Scottish steel magnate, Andrew Carnegie. In keeping with the times, several years ago the library had been modernized. Glass panelled front doors, turnstiles and water sprinklers in the ceiling had been added. Computers and wall to wall carpeting had helped to bring the library into the 21st century.

This morning, head librarian, Mrs. Ida Proudfoot her tortoise shell rimmed glasses dangling from a gold chain around her neck, was bending over a book cart busily resorting books into order by call number, her heavy bosom softly brushing across the spines of the books, making her nipples erect, making her feel irritable.

"What is this doing here?" She plucked out one book and then another. "Who sorted these?" she crossly asked.

Mildred Lemon, a librarian assistant, stood beside her, twisting her fingers, too upset to say a word. She had spent the previous hour struggling to get the books on the cart in correct order. Some of the numbers had worn away and it was hard to make them out. Her eyesight wasn't as good as it used to be.

Hearing footsteps, Mrs. Proudfoot signalled to Mildred to get on with it, while she herself, scuttled to her seat behind the front desk.

Pushing himself through the clicking turnstile, David headed towards her.

"Have you come to see us about an overdue book?"

Mrs. Proudfoot flirtatiously waggled her fat finger at him. "You naughty boy."

David stared at her.

"Because it's the season of good will," she trilled, "we will not be imposing a fine." Mrs. Proudfoot beamed her radar smile at him. "Here, have a chocolate that a grateful borrower brought in." She reached into her desk and pulled out a box. She extended it towards David and, at the same time, helped herself to one, murmuring, "Mm, delicious. I'm a naughty girl to eat one so early in the morning."

David ignored the chocolates. "Madam, I'm here on a murder investigation." He dropped his ID on her desk, so that she would have to put her glasses on to read it. How condescending. No matter how many times he had come into the library, he knew that she could never remember his name which was a perverse form of rudeness.

"Oh, my, how exciting!" exclaimed Mrs. Proudfoot. "We have a great number of murder mysteries on our shelves by Ruth Rendell, P.D. James and Agatha Christie, but nothing like the real thing. Do you really think that I can be of help?" She coyly emphasized the 'I'.

"One of your employees was found murdered this morning." David waited to see her reaction. There was none. Maybe the idea hadn't sunk in?

"The only person who is absent is Cathy. She usually phones in when she's late. It can't be her."

"Cathy Snifton's frozen body was found down by the lake," replied David. "It looks like a homicide."

Mrs. Proudfoot took a deep breath, then a startled, "Surely, not here in Mariposa?"

"Murder has no preference. It can happen anywhere."

"How perfectly dreadful. It's hard to imagine anyone doing such a thing. Poor dear, so young," sighed Mrs. Proudfoot. She took a delicate lace Swiss hanky out of her sleeve, fluffed it open dramatically before touching it to a corner of her right eye. But tears did not come.

Poor Cathy, thought David, no real sign of grief here either.

"Can you tell me about her habits? Where did she go to

lunch? Who were her friends at work? I'll need to speak to them."

"Cathy brought her lunch in a brown paper bag." Mrs. Proudfoot rolled her eyes at the ceiling. "She was keen on health foods—tabbouleh salad, whole grain bread and carrot sticks. She put her packed lunch into the staff lounge refrigerator as soon as she'd arrive. She never drank coffee. She said there was too much caffeine in it.

"I stopped asking her if she would like a nice cup of Earl Grey tea I prepared for our tea break. She always turned up her nose saying that there was almost as much caffeine in the tea as there was in the coffee. Cathy," declared Mrs. Proudfoot sarcastically, "preferred herbal teas. She made her own pot of tea with the library kettle. Earl Grey wasn't good enough for her."

"Where did Cathy go on her lunch hour?"

"On sunny days she liked to go for a walk, sit in the park or out on the library lawn. Lately she said that she was just going for a walk—for exercise and to get some oxygen into her brain."

"Did Miss Snifton have any enemies?"

"Sniff," she smiled, "that's what we called her around here because of her many colds. Well they weren't actually colds, more like post nasal drip." said Mrs. Proudfoot, laughing at her little joke. "I can't imagine Sniff as having any enemies unless she breathed on one of our elderly book borrowers and gave him pneumonia. She was hardly the type to inspire violent emotions in anyone. If you know what I mean."

"Did you notice anything unusual before Friday?"

"Sniff was very much her own person. A fragile outward appearance but a fierce spirit of independence. She kept her affairs pretty much to herself. In the morning when she'd arrive, she'd hang that big down coat of hers up over there on that hook."

David glanced over to where she pointed.

"That coat of hers was thick enough to keep two people warm. That mohair scarf of hers she never took it off. She usually wore it to protect that delicate neck of hers from drafts. What drafts, I'd asked her. Drafts, she had said firmly."

David considered the irony of her words, then asked, "What about her private life?"

Mrs. Proudfoot sighed. "Sniff was very discreet about her private life. She lived with her widowed mother who was crippled with arthritis. An old harridan if you ask me. Although, Sniff never came right out and said so. But I gathered from other people that she made things difficult for Sniff. The story I heard was that Sniff was her only daughter. Several years ago, over some family disagreement, her brother had run off. They haven't heard from him since."

"Did her mother ever come into the library?"

"Never. Sniff sometimes took books home to her."

"Who took Cathy's phone calls when she wasn't here?"

"Mildred did. Twice I took the calls. One was a young male voice asking for Cathy. The other caller, as I remember, had an older, more cultivated voice. I told him she was out. Did he want to leave his name? No. Could he leave a message? No. He would call again when she returned. Thank you very much. She never discussed with us who they were. She never addressed them by name. Cathy was very discreet about her private life. Not that she had much, living with that demanding mother of hers. It would be hard to bring friends back to that place. They wouldn't be welcome. No one has been inside that place for years."

"Do you know if Cathy was the sole support of her mother?" asked David.

"Her mother had a small widow's pension. I don't think it was very much. Look at the state of that once lovely house, it's gone to pot. It's a shame."

A heavy book came crashing down to the floor from the shelves to the right of Mrs. Proudfoot's desk. David looked into the dark, troubled eyes of Mildred Lemon as she stepped out from the shelves and knelt to retrieve the book.

"Oh how clumsy of me," she blushed. "I'm all thumbs today."

David thought. She's been listening. She knows something. "May I have a few words with Mildred?" asked David.

"Certainly, if you really think it will be of any help." Mrs. Proudfoot arched her eyebrows. "I'll take my break now and leave you two alone." She pushed back her chair and walked down the hall to the staff lounge.

Mildred watched her retreating figure until it was out of sight, then she turned expectantly towards him.

"Can we find somewhere to talk quietly?" asked David, "so that we won't be overheard."

"Well, um, um, perhaps over there in the library's *Quiet Corner* by the window. There are two chairs for reading. We won't be bothering anyone at this time in the morning. No one comes into the library this early to read." Mildred led the way. Then she sat down and nervously twisted her long thin fingers back and forth in her lap. She waited for David to begin.

"Your colleague, Cathy Snifton, was found dead this morning. Her frozen body was found down by the lake. She was murdered."

"Oh, no," said Mildred with an agonised look. "Not Cathy, not her! I overhead you talking but I didn't realize it was her. I thought it was someone else." Tears welled up in her eyes. She began to weep softly and then louder, a big wave of pain convulsing through her thin body.

"Forgive me, forgive my tears. I feel so foolish, crying in front of a stranger. But Cathy was nice to me. She made working here bearable." She sobbed.

David waited for Mildred to regain her dignity. He welcomed this first sign of genuine grief shown by anyone for the dead girl. Someone cared. But what could Cathy, a young woman and this dreary middle-aged woman in a long sleeved cardigan, tweed skirt and brogues have in common, he wondered?

"Can you tell me about yesterday? It could help a great deal if you could. Take your time and try to remember everything that happened."

Mildred coughed to clear her throat.

"Cathy and I were on the front desk together. Mrs. Proudfoot was absent for several hours to attend a Christmas luncheon.

"We did the usual, take in books, stamp the outgoing

ones, answer questions on where to locate a certain book. Mrs. Proudfoot doesn't like me using the computer. She thinks that I will wreck it. The public use it all the time to find call numbers. Why shouldn't I?

"During a lull in the afternoon, we sat down to have a little chat. Cathy asked me what I was doing for Christmas. I was hoping that she'd ask me over to her house—like she did last year. But my hopes were dashed when Cathy said that she didn't know what she was going to do this year. She told me that she had no plans which was a complete surprise to me. I had counted on going there so much. I had no one else to share Christmas with. Her mother didn't bother me. I got along with her. I hoped by not saying anything or pressing Cathy, that things would be like they were." A tear slid down Mildred's cheek.

"Did she seem different lately?" asked David.

"Yes, she wasn't concentrating on what I was saying when I was speaking to her. Kept staring off into space. She wasn't her usual self. I could tell something was bothering her."

"Did she get any phone calls?"

"Yes. While Cathy was in the washroom, the phone rang. A strong male voice demanded, 'Cathy, can she come to the phone?'

"I went and got her. I heard her say something like. I explained to you for the umpteenth time, I don't like you calling me here at work. How many times do I have to tell you? There was a pause and then she said, 'Yes, yes, I'll meet you,' in a resigned sort of way."

"Did you catch where or when she was going to meet that person?"

"No."

"Have you heard that voice before?"

"I've been thinking about that while we've been talking. Yes, I may have heard him call a couple of times before, but not lately."

"Have you any idea at all who it was?"

"None," said Mildred shaking her head. "About three o'clock, Mrs. Proudfoot sailed in on cloud nine, a trifle merry after a liquid lunch. About this time, Cathy got another call. At first she flirted with the caller, then she turned serious. But I didn't catch what she was saying. Mrs. Proudfoot was badgering me about the neatness of the shelves again."

"Did she tell you anything about that caller?"

"Nothing. I didn't want to intrude on Cathy's privacy. I valued her friendship and I wanted to keep it."

"Did you see her leave on Friday?"

"Yes, we were in the ladies' washroom together. Cathy was chatting away about nothing really, about going shopping for groceries on Saturday at the market and maybe later buying a new dress. I didn't pay much attention. But I noticed her face had more colour. She also put some eye shadow on and a dab of lipstick. She usually doesn't wear eye shadow to work. Then she took some cologne out of her purse and touched it to her throat, wrists and thighs. 'Have a nice weekend, Mildred.' That was the last thing she ever said to me."

"You assumed that she was going to meet a man?"

"Yes," said Mildred quietly. "Yes, her mood was happier, lighter. Usually she is more subdued."

David paused before saying, "Whoever she was going to meet probably was her killer." He kept his eyes riveted on her face to see her reaction.

Mildred sighed. "I thought of that too, that's why I'm trying so hard to remember everything. But there's no more to tell."

"If you can think of anything, recall something unusual, or out of the ordinary, give me a call, please." David handed her his card.

She took it. "Cathy was too young to die. She didn't deserve this."

David nodded. He had heard that sentiment before. "Courage is for the living," said David, as he left a weeping Miss Lemon dabbing at her red eyes.

Walking to his car, David thought, this Saturday morning has been a real downer. He headed straight to his office to see if there were any messages and to look again at his notes.

Chapter 2

After a quick lunch of broccoli soup and a banana muffin at Apple Annie's, David drove down to the lake again to see if he had missed something. This time, he would be alone without the prying eyes of the newspaper reporter and the freelance videographer for Barrie TV station. He could pay more attention without his colleagues yapping in the background. He needed to concentrate.

He drove down Mississauga and took a left to reach the park. Today there were only three cars in the parking lot. It was noon, everyone would be home for lunch. First he would stop at the skating rink which was part of the lake but close to the shore, protected from the strength of the waves by concrete breakers. In summer it was where everyone in Mariposa went swimming. Those crazy, lazy days of summer when he liked to get in a few swan dives off the diving board at the edge of the pier. Swan dives? More like belly flops he had to admit.

Above the skating rink, the loudspeaker attached to the telephone pole was playing the 'The Skaters' Waltz'. How ironic, he thought. The same piece that Cathy's music box played in her bedroom. It gave him a creepy feeling. He could picture Cathy twirling around in her flashing silver skates, her red mohair scarf trailing behind her, circling the ice with her friends, laughing, calling out to them.

She must have felt free here, he thought, away from her mother and that house, away from the library and the nasty Mrs. Proudfoot. He watched the few skaters circle the ice. One of them could be the killer. Oh, come on, David, that's too farfetched. You're letting your imagination run away with you. These skaters were only parents out skating with their children.

The music stopped. Over the loudspeaker came the announcement, "Please clear the rink. Workmen will be icing the rink for the next fifteen minutes."

David walked over to speak to Tim, the rink guard, who was busy shooing the skaters off the edge of the rink, keeping them clear of the ice machine.

"Hi, Tim. When you have a minute, I want to ask you a

few questions?"

"Sure thing. Just let me get the rink cleared and I'll be with you."

David waited patiently at the edge of the rink until Tim was free. "I have a picture of a young woman, about twenty-three years of age, but she looks a lot younger without make up. Do you recognize her?"

"Sure I recognize her. She skated here in the evenings. Is there something wrong?"

"Suspicious death. She was found frozen this morning at the edge of the lake." David pointed in that direction.

"Wow! Right here in the park? Nothing like that has ever happened around here. It's kind of scary."

"What did you know about her? How often did she come down here?"

"She used to come down here about two or three times a week. She and her friends used to put on their skates over there," he pointed to a bench. "Or else they went to the warming hut to change. It's too bad. She was a nice girl. It's hard to imagine something like that happening to her."

"Did you ever get a chance to talk to her?"

"Just to say hi, and nothing else."

"Do you remember any of her friends?"

"Yeah. Some of them."

"Describe them." David took out his notebook.

"There was a good looking guy, with a tan. He was very popular with the chicks. Tom Ball, his dad owns the Ball Haberdashery store on Mississauga. Then there was another guy, a bit of a wimp. I didn't take to him at all. I heard someone call out his name, James, I think it was. There was also a pretty girl, but she wasn't as flashy as Cathy. Cathy had more flash. Clara, that's her. That's the one."

David nodded. "Did you notice anything unusual last night? Did you hear any shouting, any noise that you can remember that was different?"

"Can't say it was that different." said Tim, "It was like any other Friday night with the usual Friday night crowds— teens, and young couples and the singles. Mm. I don't recall seeing Cathy, though."

"Are you sure?"

"Yeah, I'm sure. The lights and the music stopped at 10:00 p.m. I couldn't be one hundred per cent sure. But I think I could remember her if I did."

"When you left the rink what direction did you walk through the park?"

"About 10,30 p.m. or a little after, I walked towards the parking lot and then through the far end and then up Mississauga. I didn't see any of Cathy's crowd."

"Did you see anyone at all?"

"The place was pretty deserted, except for couples parked in their cars. To save myself a lot of trouble, I mind my own business and just concentrate on skating."

"If anything jogs your memory, give me a call." David handed him his card. "If you recall anything at all, no matter how unimportant you think it is, I would appreciate hearing from you."

David set off across the rink to the edge of the lake and then out onto the breakers. By walking on top of the cement breakers, he avoided walking on the ice, slippery at the best of times. At the far end was the small island, less than six and a half miles long with enough soil for two lonely wind beaten pine trees to exist. Not room enough to be a good hiding place or a place to meet, David decided. He continued walking a few more feet to the spot where he had found her. That was easy, the yellow tape ringing the trees was still there.

Why did it happen at the edge of the lake? So isolated, so cut off from the beaten path. She must have come through the park like I did, that would have been the easiest way. But why there? Her body hadn't been dragged there and left. No signs on the body to indicate that.

Whoever did it, didn't want the body to be discovered for a while. In an early spring thaw, her body would have sunk to the bottom of the lake or else she would have been eaten by foraging wild animals. Several months from now, there would only be bones. It was just luck that I noticed the scarf. Why was she strangled? Why wasn't she shot or stabbed or knocked unconscious with something. Why the scarf? Was it because it was handy? There were so many questions that he would have to find the answers to. As soon as he got back to the office, he would start interviewing her friends.

When he finally got back to the office, David put his feet up on the desk and took out his notebook, to reread his own hand writing, almost illegible at times, he admitted, even to himself. Then he flicked on the radio to catch, *'News flash Early this morning, frozen female body found by lake. Foul play is suspected.'* David switched the radio off.

What he needed now was a hot cup of Java, caffeine to stimulate his brain. There had been no murder investigation in Mariposa in the two years he'd been here. The only local action had been a little break and enter, drunk and disorderly conduct in a public place and theft.

The last incident that he covered was when a farmer out in the township beat up the little woman and then strangled the family cat. When David asked him why he did it, the farmer's quick reply was, wasn't it lucky it wasn't the other way around, strangled the wife and beat up the cat.

David remembered reading an analysis of *Who Murders Who* by Neil Boyd. The author's conclusion was that most murders that occur are either alcohol or drug related and take place in families or in family situations, with your nearest and dearest most likely to do you in. Men kill for a variety of reasons, but for the small proportion of women that kill—the predominant motive—is passion. A very small percentage, ten percent are committed by a stranger. Cathy Snifton's murder could be a murder of opportunity, being at the wrong place or the wrong time. Oh come on, what was she doing at the edge of the lake at midnight on a Friday night in freezing weather?

"How am I going to sort all this out?" David asked himself. Would he have to interview everyone in town? He smacked himself on the forehead. Don't get your balls in an uproar. Steady does it. First deal with the known. Interview her friends. Find out what kind of a person she was and how her friends fitted into her life. Find out who her enemies were. She must have had some. Who would have reason to kill her?

Think of the murder as some sort of puzzle. What had the deceased done or was doing that had been so threatening that the murderer was compelled to do something. What was so threatening in Cathy's background that she had to be killed.

David picked up the photographs of the death scene. Under the glare of the police search lights, the black and white glossy prints took on a surreal quality. The murder scene looked like life on the face of the moon or some obscure planet.

Everywhere there was the whiteness of snow, with its shades and shadows of grey, and the glitter of ice. There were several close-ups of the body and several of the position of the body in relation to the edge of the island and the shore. David peered closer. The astronauts in the exploded space vessel, 'The Challenger' had been identified by their footprints. here were no indentations in the snow, no tell-tale footprints, that could determine weight and sex. The wind had taken care of that, that and a fresh snowfall.

David had hoped that the photographs would show him something that he had missed. But he could see nothing more, except to the right, the tall pine trees on that tiny island bending in the high wind.

David leaned back in his chair to reflect on the case, when a snowball smacked the glass pane in front of him. Going over to the window, he glanced down to see rosy cheeked Mira Smith, framed by her white fur-lined parka, standing in the snow below. The men in the town referred to the divorced Mrs. Smith, the local reporter for the Mariposa Packet and Times, as 'Eat 'em alive, Mira'.

"I'm coming in," waved Mira, gesturing to him that she wanted to see him.

David's first impulse was to tell her to get lost. But he could ill afford to offend the press with a murderer running loose in Mariposa. Besides, Mira might prove useful.

"Mira," he said with exaggerated politeness. "Do come in. You're just in time for coffee."

"That's what I like to hear," said Mira, taking off her parka so he could get a good look at her figure, enhanced by her tight v-neck angora sweater and jeans. She handed her coat to David who quickly took it and went to the hall and hung it up.

Then he pulled up a chair by the desk for her to sit down

on. But Mira chose instead to perch on the edge of his desk, at such an angle, that David without any effort at all could peer down the deep cleavage between her heavy breasts.

Mira licked her top lip. "Mr. Scott, you have been most uncooperative. The police and our newspaper, I believe, have always worked hand in hand to SERVE THE COMMUNITY."

"Mira, please, call me, David," said David mockingly, trying hard to avoid looking at her voluptuous breasts. "I have to protect my reputation and be circumspect. I have to proceed," he drummed on the desk top with his fingers, "I have to proceed with caution." He grinned, "I don't want a sexual harassment charge brought against me."

Mira threw back her head and laughed, "Oh, you men are all the same."

"Oh, yeah, but are you women all the same?" retorted David.

"Off the pot," said Mira, changing the subject. "Come out with it. What have you found out so far? Huh?"

David laughed. Mira was coming on strong as usual.

"Mira," he said placatingly, "I have your interests at heart. Because I value you and respect you." He took her hand off his thigh, as he felt his face redden and felt also the heat in his groin. Gawd this woman is pushy. She is trying to give me a hard on, so that I will give her a scoop.

"You're jumping the gun, Mira. We have a murderer in our town. He may be a friend of Cathy's or he may be a stranger who killed because of opportunity and on impulse. There's not much to go on. There's no tracks in the snow. No witnesses. It's an isolated spot on the lakeshore, at the far edge of the park. It occurred between 11 p.m. and 1 a.m. We won't have the exact time of death until the pathologist's report comes in. The investigation is just in the preliminary stages."

"What did Cathy's mother say?"

"When I went to inform Mrs. Snifton that her daughter had met with foul play, she hadn't realised that her daughter hadn't come home that night. She thought that Cathy had just slept in. Mrs. Snifton was in a state of shock. Cathy was such a good girl, she told me, why would anyone want to murder her?"

"Only good girls get murdered," replied Mira, running her long scarlet fingernail through the hairs on the back of his hand. "Bad girls live to a ripe old age, like me."

"Cute." said David. Privately he thought, Mira has got it all added up. I'm sexually vulnerable and as lonely as hell. Be careful! It's a landmine.

"Mira, I'll keep you informed. Trust me." He stood up to signal that their conversation was over. "I have got to get some rest for tomorrow when I go out and interview all of Cathy's friends, a chore that I'm not looking forward to."

"All work and no play will make David a very dull boy," replied Mira coolly giving David a long, lingering look.

"Yeah, I heard that one," replied David, "How about this one? The early bird gets the worm!"

"Who wants the worm!" retorted Mira closing the door behind her.

Chapter 3

On Monday morning, the thermostat outside David's living room plunged to a chilling 25 degrees below zero. David whistled. He opened the front door and snatched the morning paper from the mat outside the door. In large headlines, he read, '*Few Clues. Police have few clues in their search for the killer of Cathy Snifton, the young librarian whose body was found early Saturday morning.*' David went on to read how the victim would be missed by her colleagues at Mariposa Public Library and the Mariposa United Church Choir. The article went on to interview Cathy's close friend, Clara Clarke, who tearfully commented, "Cathy was a wonderful person. Who would want to do such a thing? I feel that I have lost my closest friend."

Mira's article closed with an appeal to the public. The police needed their help in ascertaining the victim's movements between 7 p.m. and 1 a.m. on the evening of Friday, December 13th. Anyone who had seen Cathy Snifton or seen anything unusual that evening near the lake at the edge of the park was asked to contact Dave Scott of Mariposa O.P.P. who would be assisting Bob White in the investigation. The phone number followed.

"Thanks, Mira," said David silently.

When David arrived at the office, he was no sooner seated at his desk, when Clancy popped his head around the corner. "Just thought, I'd let you know. Bob White called from Barrie. He can't handle the investigation yet. He wants you," Clancy patted Dave on the back, "to continue. My guess, Davie, my boy, he won't be available for a while. It's a jungle down there in Barrie." He winked at David, "Take your time. Don't rush things. No false arrests, huh?"

David scowled. "You mean that I am going to have to go it alone. Thanks a lot, pal."

"Ah," said Clancy, "don't get your shorts tied in a knot. White just can't get over here yet is all that I'm saying. Don't make a big thing out of it. Easy does it."

"Sure, pal of mine," said David, sarcastically.

"Davie, Davie," said Clancy, shaking his head, "we'll give you back up."

"That's what they all say."

Thanks to Mira's article, the phone calls trickled in. Some were helpful, others were not. Most were not. But even the calls that appeared to have no connection with the case had to be listened to, for good public relations sake in a small town. No one said that it would be easy. There were a lot of kooks and cranks out there and they all had to have their say. David leaned back in his chair and placed his feet up on the desk.

The phone rang again. David reached over and picked up the receiver. "Are you David Scott?"

"Yes, ma'am. What can I do for you?" It was the voice of an old woman.

"My name is Miss Temple and I need your help."

"What seems to be the problem?" David closed his eyes and leaned back in his chair.

"I have been receiving several threatening phone calls."

Every old lady who calls us, thought David, gets funny phone calls. They never blame it on being hard of hearing.

"Tell me about it," sighed David.

"When I pick up the phone, I keep asking, 'Hello, hello, who is it?' I know someone is there. Sometimes it is just heavy breathing. But last night a male caller said, 'You'd better keep your nose out of what doesn't concern you or you'll wind up dead.'"

Probably the next door neighbour telling her to butt out. "What kind of a voice did he have? Young? Old? An accent?"

"He didn't sound old. He didn't speak with an accent."

"Do you have any enemies?"

"Sir, my dealings with people in general have been most congenial. Really! The idea!" But then she paused. Her voice quavered. "Ever since that young girl has been murdered, no one in Mariposa is safe. I got a call again last night. I don't know what to do. Bell is no help. They won't put a tap on my line. They won't do anything until I have had twenty calls. They told me, just take down the time these calls are made and the message. I might be dead by then. They want me to pay for call display. I'm

32

on a fixed pension. I can't afford it. Can't you do something?"

David rubbed his red his eyes and looked at his watch. It might be a good time to take a break and get out of the office. Visit the old girl for some light relief. "How about I drop over to see you and take all the details down. Your address?"

David drove over to Miss Temple's home. It was a small one-storey cottage, now almost dwarfed by snow drifts. Coming up the shovelled walk, he could see a short grey haired old woman with sharp eyes peering out the window at him. She must have been eighty at least. But with grey hair, it's hard to tell. At the door, she greeted him with a brisk cheerful, "Come in, come in. Close the door quickly behind you. It's a cold day."

"Colder than most, ma'am." David took off his hat.

"It was good of you to come."

Miss Temple led him quickly into the living room where the sun was pouring through the windows. Some plant boxes had been placed on a small table in front of the window.

Curious, David asked her, "What are you growing?"

"Are you interested in growing things? I am," beamed Miss Temple proudly. "These are my pride and joy. It's a long, seedless European cucumber—a special kind of cucumber. It needs no bees for fertilization. It bears fruit without fertilization. It is parthenocarpic."

"Huh?" said David, wondering what the old girl was leading up to.

"In the Bible, there is a good example. That is, if you read your Bible?" Miss Temple raised her eyes to meet his. "The Immaculate Conception. The Virgin Mary and Jesus who had no earthly father. That's a Biblical example. Do you know that plants are sexual? There are males—stamens)—and females—pistils—the anthers, the testes; the pollen, the sperm; the stigma, the vulva; the style, the vagina, the ovary and the seed. Now do you understand how unusual these cucumbers are that I am growing?"

"Yes, indeed Ma'am." Migawd, thought David, a lecture on sex and plants. I'm not here for this. "Let's stick to the facts, Ma'am. I'm here because of your complaints about several threatening phone calls. It would help, Ma'am if you would try to see if they fit any pattern. Do they always call at the same time of day or evening? Instead of answering the phone yourself, put on your answering machine and tape the calls. Your caller might just hang up and get tired of not reaching you. Some nuts get a kick out of the listener's reactions. Try to get his voice on tape. Do you think that you can do that?"

"I can try. But you know what this means. I will have to go out and buy some contraption and hook it up to my phone. None of my friends uses answering machines. They say it's too impersonal. All this fuss is hard on my heart. I don't know whether my heart can stand it," said Miss Temple putting her hand on her thin bony chest. "It flutters so easily."

David nodded.

"Another thing I wanted to tell you before it slips my mind. The night that girl was murdered, we had a full moon. While I was gazing at it out of the living room window, a man came out of the bushes and dropped his trousers right in front of my window. It was disgusting. Revolting!"

David bit hard on his lip. He could hardly keep from smiling. Someone was just having a public crap after a party and decided to show off by doing it on some old lady's front lawn. In this freezing temperature, he'd have to be fast or suffer the consequences of frostbite.

"Did you get a good look at his face? Do you remember any noticeable characteristics?"

"How could I? I was too upset, too flustered to notice anything. Just what are you going to do?" demanded Miss Temple shoving her face into his. "What are you prepared to do about the exposure of male genitalia on my front lawn? Do you think the two things are related—the threatening phone calls and that display?"

"No, Ma'am. I don't think that they are related. Bring us in a recording tape and we'll have something to work on. Okay?"

"I'm not mechanically minded, twiddling knobs and that sort of thing. But if you insist. I thought that there might be a simpler solution."

"These things take time. Ma'am. Time. Rome wasn't built in day." replied David, putting on his hat preparing to leave.

"Time isn't on my side," said Miss Temple, with pursed

lips. David could see that she wasn't pleased with his advice at all.

He had tried to be helpful and all he had gotten was vim and vinegar, he thought as he got back into his car. Not a sweet old lady at all.

Chapter 4

Over at the United Church Manse, Reverend Billy Day had slept in late. He carefully dumped the crumbs from his toast in the garbage can and then took his breakfast dishes to the sink. It was hard to keep from yawning. He wanted to clear his head before going over the draft for his Sunday sermon. But his head was throbbing. Fresh air and a jog was the only cure. He went out into the hall. Putting on his wool toque, he noticed a slight bump at the back of his head. That's strange. How did that get there? He put on his gloves, tucked in his scarf and carefully zipped up his jacket. It was going to be another cold day. Before leaving he hollered up the stairs, "I'm off now, Mabel. I won't be home until this evening." Mabel didn't reply. Probably didn't hear him. He shut the door securely and headed down the walk.

In his Gore-Tex blue jogging suit, tall and trim, 45-year-old Reverend Billy Day felt relaxed and happy, just an ordinary jock out for a morning run. He had recently taken up jogging when he'd looked down and noticed a pot belly. Now that he had lost weight from jogging, he wanted to keep the habit up because of the good feeling it gave him. When he wore his white clerical collar, it was more off-putting. He noticed that when he was more formally dressed, the conversation died, the laughter stopped. His parishioners spoke in solemn terms of what they thought he wanted to hear. Didn't they realize that Billy like to laugh and even God liked to laugh. Although lately there hadn't been much to laugh about.

A four-kilometre jog through Mariposa would give him the energy to tackle his sermon, to stimulate some ideas before checking into his study. Later he would jog home, pick up his car and then return for the rest of the day.

Ahead of him on the walk, Billy recognized a tiny figure trudging carefully through the snow towards him. It was Miss Temple, one of God's unclaimed treasures. She was wearing her usual winter outfit, a thin black wool coat which clung to her small frame and a moth eaten leopard tam perched precariously on one side of her head. When he had first commented on her fashionable hat, she had told him proudly that it was made of real leopard, none of that artificial polyester stuff. Where Billy wondered had she been able to get her hands on real leopard? In one hand Miss Temple held her string carry-all.

Miss Temple reminded Billy of his dear, departed mother. When she stood almost in front of him on the path he couldn't check the impulse. He bent over and gently planted a kiss on her forehead. But she moved at the last second, and his kiss landed on the tip of her nose.

Stepping back, Miss Temple squeaked a surprised, "Well, really!"

For an embarrassing moment, Billy thought he had left his fly open. He looked down at his crotch. Reassured that there was no fly in his sweat pants and no protruding boner in his groin he shook his head. Old ladies get such queer ideas over an innocent gesture. It was probably the first kiss that she had received in a long time. Silly Miss Temple. Poor, lonely old soul is desperate for affection, but does not know how to graciously accept it. He peered inside her carry all. He saw a loaf of whole wheat bread, a carton of two percent milk, a tin of cat food and a package of frozen Brussels sprouts.

"Can I help you in any way, dear Miss Temple? Can I carry some of your parcels?"

"Please," said Miss Temple, angrily straightening herself up to her full height of one and a half metres. With a crisp, "I am doing very well, thank you. It won't be necessary. I am perfectly capable of carrying my own parcels, Reverend Day, perfectly capable. I am not some poor old thing that can't carry her own parcels. I am certainly not a person who can be pigeon-holed as old and helpless and shoved into a corner."

"Who would do that? Surely no one would want to do that to you," said Billy trying to humour her. "Where are you going to spend Christmas, Miss Temple?"

"I am going to spend Christmas Day with someone that means a great deal to me, someone very special."

"Oh, ho" thought Billy, his curiosity aroused. Does she

have a special male friend that I haven't heard about? This surprised him because he envisioned Miss Temple spending Christmas Day alone at home in her little cottage.

"Dr. Sandy and his family were hoping to have you over for Christmas dinner. They told me that they would love to have you."

"That is very kind of them, but I will have to decline. I am having dinner with Diefenbaker."

"Who?" shouted Billy, thinking the old lady's brains were really scrambled. "The late prime minister?" he said to humour her.

"No, don't be silly. My favourite cat, Diefenbaker."

"Miss Temple," said Billy gravely, "sharing Christmas dinner with a cat is not as emotionally rewarding an experience as sharing dinner with a loving family. A cat is not a human being. Dr. Sandy told me that he wanted you to come and join them."

"It's kind of them," said Miss Temple proudly, "but I will have to decline."

Oh, thought Billy. Is she crazy? Who would want to decline a lovely meal at Dr. Sandy's? He would jump at the chance.

Billy resumed his jogging. To give his route more variety, he turned into Mississauga with its bright Christmas lights and wreaths hung up on lamp posts. He could hear the loudspeakers playing Christmas carols as he jogged along. Where has my enthusiasm for Christmas gone? Where is my joy? All the mud and snow blocking his path further added to his depression.

Approaching Apple Annie's he smelled their freshly baked muffins. The smells were intoxicating. He had tasted them all—carrot, banana, cranberry and blueberry. He resisted the temptation to sit down and have a cup of coffee and a fresh home baked muffin. Something he never got at home! But he had already had two cups of coffee, enough caffeine for now.

He noticed Tom Ball shovelling snow out in front of his father's store. Usually Tom engaged in some pleasant chit chat, but today Tom avoided looking at him. Not like him, not like him at all.

Billy pressed on. His breath blew out in front of him like little white clouds. Under his track suit he was sweating. It was becoming hard going. Most of the walks had been cleared by the city, but here and there he had to jog in the street before getting back onto the sidewalk.

Christmas this year was going to be like any other day. He felt no enthusiasm. Mabel had decided Christmas dinner would be fish like those of the early Christians. Fish served on a white plate alongside white boiled potatoes and white turnip. How he craved a Christmas dinner like those he remembered from his childhood, with a succulent fat Butterball turkey sitting on an enormous platter surrounded by roast potatoes, squash, turnip, peas and carrots, stuffing with raisins and oregano, glorious fattening gravy and then polished off with steamed Christmas pudding with lots of plum sauce. He sighed thinking of the past.

But it was more than Christmas dinner that he missed. Deep inside, he felt empty. He'd spent all his time listening to other people's problems, their difficulties, their pain and he'd denied that he had any himself. He hadn't had time for himself and he hadn't had time for Mabel.

He pictured tall, big boned Mabel, with her pepper coloured hair. She reminded him now more and more of his mother. She looked old and he felt old beside her. How can I tell Mabel that we are dancing the slow steps of death?

His throat was dry. He needed a drink of water. Should he turn back to Mississauga Street and the water fountain besides the library? No, it would be better to keep going and to stop at one of the parishioner's houses.

He was now in front of the Chirp house. Happy, cheerful, Gale Chirp sang in the church choir. She had always reminded him of that childhood nursery rhyme, 'Cheerie, cheerie, chee. I'm a happy Robin Red Breast, singing in the tree.' He had heard that their marriage was in trouble. By dropping by and asking for a drink of water, he'd be able to offer his help and inquire as to how they were doing.

Billy rang the bell. After what seemed like an eternity, standing there in the cold, wondering if anyone was home, he saw the door open slightly. Behind it, he heard the softly whispered voice, "Who's there?"

"It's me, Reverend Day."

The door swung open to reveal a thirty-year-old woman in a pink pant suit with one eye swollen shut and the other eye only half open. Her lip was cut in several places. Billy was shocked to see her in such a state.

"I'm terribly sorry to bother you, Gale. Is there anything I can do to help? I was just jogging by and I felt thirsty. I can come back at another time."

"Oh, Billy, I desperately need someone to talk to," and then Gale burst into tears.

"There, there," said Billy putting his hand on her shoulder.

Gale led him into a darkened living room. The room was a mess, the obvious aftermath of a fight. Newspapers had been torn and scattered across the rug. A floor lamp was lying on one side. Books and papers were strewn about. An ashtray with cigarette butts had been overturned onto the rug.

"I can't see well enough to straighten up the mess. Billy, you're the only one I can turn to. Look at me. My face is ruined. I can't take it anymore."

"Sit down, please, Gale and tell me all about it."

Gale leaned against him. "Oh, Billy, what am I going to do?" Another burst of tears and then Gale buried her soft blonde head of curls in his lap, his crotch to be more precise, and this had a very disconcerting effect on Billy. He should have remained standing. But how was he to foresee that Gale was going to bury her head in his groin? The poor distraught woman didn't realize that it was causing him to have an embarrassing erection. Billy decided to ignore his own discomfort and to put his hand down and stroke that lovely head of curls. He was surprised by its softness. His wife's hair he hardly ever wanted to touch. It was so dry and rough, like a horse's mane. Gale's hair was like a bird's nest of down.

"Everything is going to be fine, Gale."

"Oh, Billy, you're so good. So kind. I don't deserve your kindness. My husband is a good man, but he has no control over himself when he's been drinking. I have tried to be patient. I have tried to be a good wife. This is a small town. Oh Billy, I feel mortified bleating my problems to you. I have always tried to hide them. You don't know what it's like living with him.

"Lately things haven't been going well. He's come home, loaded with work saying that he had a deadline to meet. Then he'd retreat to the recreation room. I tried to keep the children quiet. I warned them. Don't bother your father. I tried to keep the house neat and tidy and to look attractive for when he came home from work. I tried to serve up the kind of meals that I knew he liked. I tried to be the perfect wife. But nothing was good enough." Gale broke into a fresh round of sobbing.

Billy patted her hand. "There, there, don't cry. Wives of abusive men, think it's all their fault. They don't realize that this violent behaviour comes within that person, regardless of any external stimulus. It's not your fault, Gale."

"Oh, I hope not," sobbed Gale. "Everything had to be so perfect. Supper had to be served up on the dot. If it was late a second, he would fly off the handle. He'd pick fault at anything, even the tiniest detail set him off. Everything had to be just so.

"In front of the children, I would cower in fear. He'd call me a whore and a bitch at the top of his lungs. I can't take it anymore! At nights, the neighbours heard me screaming and called the police. When the officers arrived and knocked on the door, my husband would greet them, all charm and personality. When they'd asked, 'Mind if we look around?' My husband would say, 'Certainly. My wife and I have just been watching TV.' I would falsely smile. What screaming? Nothing had been going on here. They looked upstairs at the children in their bedrooms asleep. Nothing unusual, nothing out of the ordinary. We were just one big, happy family. Maybe the TV was turned up too loud, my husband would suggest, or they had gotten the wrong house.

"I stood there a silent victim, Billy, because my children are young. They needed their father. I couldn't leave him and support them on my own. He made this very clear to me. Who would believe me? 'Child support,' he sneered, 'half the men in the country disappear and their wives never see a nickel. Try getting support out of me.'

"I kept hoping things would change. That things would go back to the good old days when we were first married, but they didn't. Last night we had another big row after supper. I told him that he had to get out, to sleep somewhere else for the night. I don't know what I'm going to do. I don't know how I'm going to manage."

"Take courage, Gale. No difficulty is too great that there isn't a solution," said Billy. "Such a pretty face. There should be no room for tears on such a pretty face."

Impulsively Billy swept his arms around her in a big hug. Keep it light, he warned himself. But he didn't want to let go of this fragile woman. Billy could feel his penis pressing urgently against his sweat pants. He quickly got to his feet. "Here, let me help you up." said Billy, "Things will get better, Gale. They may look bleak now, but every cloud has a silver lining. Look. I'll drop in from time to time to see how you're getting along."

"Oh, Billy, I'd be so grateful if you would," said Gale her face brightening.

Billy could see that her eyes were still bloodshot and her make up smeared but she seemed less desperate.

"Billy, you've given me hope."

"That's what I am here for," said Billy. "Give me a little smile."

"Season's Greetings," called out Gale as she closed the door after him. "See you soon."

As Billy continued to jog along, life looked better already. He felt glad that he had given Gale hope. Billy liked the peacefulness of Mariposa. Thankfully the developers had overlooked this town. He loved the large Victorian houses set back from the street, with their expansive green lawns and gardens. Mariposa had the best of both worlds. It was close enough to Toronto and the U.S. border and yet far enough from the problems concerned with urban life. Because Mariposa straddled both worlds, it attracted a large number of professionals—lawyers, doctors, architects and investors.

Billy glanced up at legal specialist, Greg Legatt's

sprawling ranch style home with the blue tarpaulin covering his outdoor pool at the side of the house. Legatt, a church elder, was one of its biggest contributors. Like most of his middle class parishioners, there was no financial need—no wolf howling at the door.

Across the street on the corner was Dr. Sandy's house. It was a lovely red brick Victorian home with a large front lawn in front now covered by snow drifts that undulated across the lawn like small hills. Two tall fir trees stood on either side of the front steps. The Sandys had tied large red bows to the top of the trees and placed tiny white lights throughout the branches.

Just several blocks more and he'd be at his office. Saturday was usually a quiet time down at Mariposa United. As soon as Billy had arrived and unzipped his jacket and run a comb through his hair, he heard a light knock at the door.

"Come in." Billy was surprised to see Miss Cassidy, the church secretary who never worked on Saturday, in her coat and hat, with a grim expression on her face. There's a bee buzzing in her knickers, thought Billy.

Miss Cassidy's voice was grim. "I popped over for a few minutes to discuss something serious with you."

Billy thought, oh, oh, with that tone of voice, she wants me to do something nasty.

"I noticed something disturbing at last Sunday's service. I saw Miss Temple take out a ball- point pen from that black hand bag of hers and cross out the word *he* and write above it, *people*. I was sitting right behind her. I could hardly believe my eyes. Miss Temple is mutilating our hymn books."

"Really?" said Billy in the most neutral tone he could muster to mask his anger.

"Our church budget doesn't cover replacing ball-point stained hymn books. Temple is damaging one every Sunday. What are we going to do about it?" Miss Cassidy had used the royal 'we' but what she really meant was what was he going to do about it? She wanted Billy to take action.

"What do you want me to do?" asked Billy.

"Speak to her. Ask her to stop it."

Billy sighed. So what if this eccentric old lady wants to

deface a couple of hymn books. Who would notice, except Miss Cassidy? Miss Cassidy had been the church secretary for over fifteen years. She was conscientious to a fault. Billy didn't want to cross her because she had a dangerous tongue. "I'll speak to her. I'll ask her why she's doing it."

Miss Cassidy beamed with satisfaction which angered Billy even more. "Well, I must be going." At the door she paused, "Oh, by the way, did you listen to your radio this morning? On the ten o'clock news there was something about the body of a young woman being found down by the lake. I didn't catch the name of the person. Did you?"

"No, no, I didn't." said Billy. "How awful. I hope it's not someone we know. I'll try to catch it on the mid-day report. They may have more details by then. Thank you for your concern, Miss Cassidy," and he ushered her firmly but quickly out of the office, glad to see the last of her.

Chapter 5

Mrs. Sandy was busily stringing popcorn, piece by piece, from a pewter bowl resting in her lap for the family Christmas tree standing in the corner of the living room. She was careful to hold the popcorn pieces in such a way that she didn't prick her finger with the needle. The house was quiet and she was alone. She was free to let her thoughts roam. Occasionally, she glanced out the window as the snowflakes floated down on the rooftops. Thankfully, it was going to be another white Christmas. She loved looking out at the flickering Christmas lights that decorated their neighbours' windows and the front door wreaths of red velvet ribbon and pine.

She got up from her chair and went over to see the thermostat attached to the wall, outside the window. Minus fifteen degrees celsius. It would be another cold night. She was glad that she was safe and sound indoors.

She thought, far off in the frozen ground of the cemetery will be Cathy Snifton's final resting place. How horrible. So young to have her life snuffed out, just before Christmas. Mrs. Sandy didn't know her well, but like everyone in Mariposa she knew her from going into the library. How helpful Cathy had been. Cathy didn't deserve to die.

Cathy had been a patient of Hal's. She remembered seeing Cathy in his office. She had asked Cathy in passing, "Are you having a good day?" She remembered Cathy saying that she was tired, no energy or pep lately. Probably flu, she'd thought. Or maybe Cathy was anaemic. She was thin enough. It was stressful looking after that mother of hers.

Just then the doorbell rang. Mrs. Sandy looked up with a nervous start. "Who can that be? Until the police solve the murder, my nerves won't be the same." She looked out through the glass panel by the door. James Muir was standing there. "Oh, no," she thought, "I forgot about sitting with his mother while he went to choir practice."

She opened the door, letting the wind whistle past her. "James, I'll be ready in a few minutes. Just let me get my coat and hat."

James stepped onto the mat inside the front door and waited. "I'm so grateful to you Mrs. Sandy for offering to look after my mother for a few hours while I'm at choir practice. You're the only one she trusts. She says she doesn't trust a stranger. You never know what they will steal. She's paranoid," said James apologetically.

"James," said Mrs. Sandy, "There are a lot of competent people who would be willing to look after your mother, like the Victorian Order of Nurses or the Home Care People. They are used to dealing with the sick and elderly."

James sadly shook his head. "I know what you're saying, Mrs. Sandy, but she doesn't want them. She just wants me, her son. She wants me to be there all the time. I try to do as much as I can. But she's so demanding. She wants me to do this and that. I try to do as much as I can. But she's so fussy. She wants everything to be done in a certain way, her way. What I do is never quite right. I am getting so I don't know how to cope anymore. I feel guilty if I don't do the things she wants me to do. But if I do everything she wants, then there is little time left over for me. Sometimes I get so angry." James twisted his gloves in his hands.

"You don't know how difficult she is. The dinner bell that she keeps on her tray, it never stops ringing. How I hate it!

"Oh forgive me, Mrs. Sandy, I don't mean to whine, but my nerves are bad tonight. I feel that I'm caught like a rat in a trap and can't get out. You're always so kind to listen to me, Mrs. Sandy. I feel awful for babbling on like this."

"Oh, James, it's nothing. I will go right over," said Mrs. Sandy reaching out her arm to James.

James' face brightened. "Everything she needs, her glass of water, her vial of pills, her tea bag and her tea pot are all on a tray in the kitchen. I also put some Laura Secord chocolates out for both of you. You'll be okay. She likes you. Thanks heaps. This choir practice means so much to me."

Poor boy, thought Mrs. Sandy watching his retreating figure. He'll get old before his time, chained to that woman. A weak heart, my eye. James will die long before she will. With his care, his mother will live to be a hundred. More than I can say for the rest of us.

She locked the door behind her and set off into the cold night. Glancing furtively behind her she noticed that she was the only one out on the street. She looked at her shadow on the snow beside her. I can't be too careful. Until that murderer is caught, I have to be alert and on my guard. Cathy would be alive today, if she'd been more careful.

*****

Monday night was usually laundry night, time to clean up the apartment. "The hell with it," thought David, kicking his boxer shorts under the bed. "I'll do it tomorrow night. I've got more important things to do than take out the garbage. I've got a murder to solve before the trail gets cold. That means going down to choir practice and getting hold of James and perhaps catching Clara at the same time."

David drove down and parked his car in the parking lot at the rear of the red brick church. The front of the church was in darkness. He found the front doors locked which was not unexpected. Walking around to the side, he found a heavy door that wasn't locked. He pulled it open. In the darkness, he stamped his feet on the rubber mat to shake off the snow. Ahead of him in the hallway, a light fixture illuminated a door. A bronze plaque read, The Reverend William Day, B.A.,D.D. Under the door he could see a light. "Mm," thought David, "it might be a good idea to have a word with him before finding the others."

Inside his study, Reverend Day was working on his Christmas sermon. What to call it? Good News? Thirst that yea may never thirst again? How about, the Immaculate Conception? He shook his head. Too Catholic. He scratched that out and decided to go with, 'Pregnant with Possibilities'.

Of all the Biblical characters, the Virgin Mary was not his favourite. His Catholic brethren thought differently. But that was their choice. Different dogma, different approach. She was too pure, too holy, too unobtainable. Untouchable. Blessed Among Women. But Mary Magdalene, she was different. He had always a certain fondness for her. She had experienced life, she wasn't a cardboard character. Like all of us, she had sinned and been forgiven.

His mind drifted away to matters concerning the church. He hoped that George had remembered to place a pail of sand next to the altar for the Christmas Eve Service. Last year, a teenage girl at the altar had set her bangs on fire when she had leaned too close to the flame to light her candle.

Christmas Day was not something he was looking forward to. It didn't feel like Christmas. Where was the excitement that he had felt as a child, the hoping, the waiting, the anticipation and the excitement and joy of the day itself?

Whose fault was it? It wasn't Mabel's fault. It wasn't his fault. We're just two grey middle-aged people living in a grey house, devoid of colour and joy. We pinch pennies financially. We switch lights off to save electricity. We keep the thermostat down to save on fuel bills. We wear heavy knit sweaters from Central America to keep us warm. To save water we take baths every other day. We buy toilet paper in bulk, so rough it feels like sandpaper. Save, save, save. But for what? We have no children.

Was there anything alive in their house? They had no pets because Mabel had allergies. They did little entertaining. People didn't drop in, because he was never home. When he was home, what did they talk about when they were together? Very little.

A knock on the door brought him back to reality.

"Who is it?" he called out. "Can't it wait until tomorrow?"

"It's Constable David Scott of the OPP. I want just a few minutes of your time."

Reverend Day opened his door just a crack. "Is something deeply troubling you, or can we put it off for a few days," inquired Billy peering out from behind the door. "I am writing my sermon."

"I didn't drop by to discuss a personal matter. I'm here to interview some choir members. Can you tell me where I can find them?"

"Come in. I don't normally see people at this hour. But it's time I took a break. When I work on my sermon, the time flies by. I get so involved."

Day was probably close to fifty, but he looked ten years younger. In front of David was an attractive, tall, clean shaven male in jogging pants and sweat shirt. He was surprised at how trim and fit the reverend was. He expected a rotund Father Brown figure, fat and balding. Exercise does it every time.

While Reverend Day shuffled his papers together on his heavy oak desk, David had a chance to get a good look around the room. It was like a large, comfortable suburban recreation room. The walls were lined with book shelves. The heavy Persian rug on the floor had a floral motif. The drawn drapes were expensive and the chair that Reverend Day had suggested that he sit in, was antique. On the wall, lit by a small light at the bottom of the frame was an oil. Christ the Good Shepherd, out on a hillside, his crook in his hand leading his flock of sheep.

"Tell me about your parishioner, Cathy Snifton. You probably heard the news. She was found murdered at the edge of the lake this morning. She sang in your choir. Tell me about who she was."

Reverend Day's face paled. He clasped his hands in front of him, then walked around to the front of his desk. "It's all very shocking that something this awful could happen to one of our flock. This is a very painful subject. She was a member of our congregation, a member of our senior choir for the last three years. She was a member of our Christian family. It's painful to talk about it." Day walked over to the draped window and stood with his hands clasped behind his back. David was disappointed that he could see only the back of his head.

"For all of us, this has been a very painful time. A member of our congregation has been cut down in the flower of her young life. Who do you think did it?"

David shrugged. "It could be anyone. Everyone is a suspect."

Reverend Day walked over to David. "That means you suspect us... people at the church... her friends in the choir...."

"Yes," said David, "I have to question everyone. No offence but where were you on Friday, December 13th between 10 p.m. and 1 a.m.?"

Reverend Day's eyes dilated. "Really officer, you don't think that I would..." he placed his hand on his breast, "that I would have wanted to murder... that I would consider murdering anyone...?"

David took out his pen and notebook. "We have to ask everyone, for the purpose of elimination."

"Well," said Day, huffily, "I was here in my study, of course. I was working on my Sunday sermon, giving it a last minute polish."

"Did anyone see you, visit or call?"

"No one," said Day. "I have no alibi. No one can vouch for me," he said softly raising his hands in a supplicating gesture, "except God."

Nothing is sacred these days, thought David, making a note of his statement. He would return later and chat to him. After all Reverend Day knew the secrets of the heart. Maybe someone would have the need to confess through guilt or remorse. That might help his investigation.

"Can you tell me where the choir is practicing?"

"Come with me and I'll show you." Reverend Day led David down the hall, through a heavy oak carved door. They ducked their heads as they entered the brightly lit choir loft.

Day coughed, and turned to David. "Maybe it would be better for you to wait in one of the pews, until the practice is over. Mr. Neary, our choirmaster, doesn't like interruptions."

They walked back through another door into the main part of the darkened church.

David slipped into a pew and looked up briefly at the stained glass windows on either side of the church which were briefly illuminated by a passing car on the street outside. It had been a long time since he had sat inside a church. He had forgotten how quiet, and how still it was. He could hear the beating of his own heart.

Ahead of him in the choir loft were the choir members, dressed in casual clothes holding their music sheets. Everyone stopped singing. He heard the irate voice of the choir master. "I want you to go over this section again. Pay attention to the second line. It isn't quite right. Some of you are coming in on the beat too late."

David coughed. Mr. Neary whirled around to face David fixing on him a frosty glare. "I didn't realize that we had an audience of one."

David stood up and identified himself and quietly said, "I'm here on business, not pleasure. After you're finished, I would like to have a word with you, along with Clara Clarke and James Muir." David sat down again.

"A traffic ticket, I suppose," snapped Neary. "It'll get paid. No problem." David saw him give a knowing wink to the choir as if to imply that David's visit to the church was a triviality. "Let's try it one more time, then call it a night."

David didn't have to wait long. Neary collected the music sheets, the other members of the choir retreated. David went up to him.

"Follow me," said Neary. "I have a small cubicle, the size of a closet where we can talk more privately."

It was a small room down the hall, just enough room for a desk a small bookshelf and piles of sheet music stacked on a table.

"Here, have a chair. I must apologize for being so abrupt. My nerves are bad," said Neary, picking up a cigarette to light. "I've been smoking and drinking too much coffee lately."

David wasn't terribly impressed by Neary's apology. His first impression was that Neary could be nice or nasty at the flip of a switch.

"I'm here to talk about Cathy Snifton who sang in your choir," said David. "She was found murdered down by the lake this morning."

"Yes, so I've heard," said Neary in a bored voice, leaning back on his chair. "Cathy was a soprano in my choir. She had a nice voice but a bit strained on the high notes. She was supposed to sing a solo at our Christmas service, but now I'll have to scrap that and find a replacement. It's dreadfully inconvenient for me at such short notice."

"I don't care whether she sang like a nightingale or a crow. I'm here to find out about Cathy and who her friends are."

"Well," sniffed Neary, "I don't see how much I can be of help. She was just a young woman who sang in my choir. You should speak to Clara and James, they were her friends. I know that James often walked her home after choir practice. They made a good pair," said Neary sarcastically, "both had mothers

51

that drove them crazy... if you know what I mean. Mothers can do that to you. My mother, on the other hand, isn't like that at all."

"I'll make a note of that," replied David sharply. What a little pouf!

"There's nothing more I can tell you." Mr. Neary picked up his brief case and began stuffing music sheets into it. "I really must go. I'll leave the door on lock and after you've interviewed those two, just shut the door behind you, please."

A thin young man stuck his head around the door. "You wanted to see me?" His Adam's apple bobbed in his throat. "I can't stay long. Mrs. Sandy is looking after my invalid mother and I have got to get back to her."

David looked closely at this tall, thin youth with thinning brown hair and grey pock-marked face with puzzlement. This was Cathy's boyfriend? Looks could be deceiving, but this combination didn't seem to gel. Something was off. But you can never judge a book by its cover.

"You heard on the news that Cathy Snifton was found murdered this morning. I need your help in finding out who killed Cathy. You were Cathy's boyfriend?"

James looked down at his feet. "I was her friend."

"How often did you meet up out with Cathy?"

"About once a week," replied James. "We," he coughed nervously into his hand, "we were just casual friends. I was very fond of her, but we weren't in love or anything like that. We were just friends."

David's ears picked up the emphasis on the word, 'just' and waited for James to speak again.

"It's hard to explain," said James. "We shared the same problem, our mothers. I had my mother, who is an invalid. Cathy's mother was crippled by arthritis. We both had demanding mothers. Cathy's mother never encouraged company. Cathy never brought anyone home. Cathy, I think was ashamed of her. Her mother rarely changed her clothes, never tried to look nice, never took an interest in the place. It was Cathy's home, too. But my mother is no angel either. She demands attention every second that I'm home. She constantly complains that nothing I do is good enough."

"Where did you go on your dates with Cathy?"

"We went to the odd movie, walks in the park, a drink down at the hotel, very casual things."

"What did you talk about?"

"Everything and anything. We both wanted to get out of Mariposa."

"Can you remember the last time you met?"

"Yes, it was Friday, the 13th. I arranged to meet Cathy and have a drink down at Brewery Bay, but she never showed up. It wasn't like her to ignore our date. She never stood me up before. Sometimes she would phone early in the afternoon and cancel saying something had come up. But she never stood me up."

"When she called and cancelled in the past, what reason did she give?"

"She would just say a she had a date and couldn't make it. Or something had come up at work and she had to stay late. Usually she couldn't get away. I should have realised something was wrong."

"How do you mean?"

"Just that. She never stood me up."

"What did you do?"

"What could I do? I felt that she would probably show up later. I was annoyed, because I had gone to the trouble to make arrangements for someone to sit with my mother. It wasn't easy. I had asked Mrs. Sandy to come over for the evening."

"Did you stay down at Brewery Bay for the rest of the evening?"

"Yes."

"Can you think of anyone that Cathy might have gone to meet?"

"No."

"Did she speak to you of any men in her life. Were you aware of her other male friends?"

James dashed David's hopes with a simple "No."

"Where were you between eleven p.m. and one a.m. that evening, James?"

James' lip trembled. "I was at home with my mother. Who else! Why ask me? I didn't do it. I swear to God, I didn't. The people in this town are talking about me behind my back and insinuating that I had something to do with her murder because I took her out. They don't come right out and say it. But they think it. How can I defend myself against the whispers when I don't know who is doing the whispering?" James looked close to tears.

"Can your mother verify this?" As soon as he uttered the question, David realized how stupid it was. Of course his mother would say he was home. But why, he wondered, if James had nothing to do with her murder, is he acting so guilty?

"Yes, my mother will confirm it." James stood up. "I've got to get back."

"Yes, of course, James." David watched the youth slip out the door, and then walked over to the door to ask Clara Clarke to come in. He found Clara quietly sitting against the wall, twisting and turning several strands of her long blonde hair over and over again in her fingers.

This girl has class written all over her, thought David, noticing the fluffy blue-green angora sweater and a single strand of pearls at her neck. Her sweater gently moulded a pair of full, round breasts. He looked into her large soft, brown eyes and his heart gave a little leap.

"Would you care to come in?" said David gently. "I have some questions I want to ask you about your friend, Cathy."

"I will do anything to help," said Clara, feasting those large brown eyes on him again. "I just can't believe it. Who would want to murder Cathy? She was one of my dearest friends. Our friendship goes back a long way. In public school when we had sleepovers, Cathy use to come and stay at our house. In High School we started to drift apart. Cathy had different friends than I did. Cathy was popular with the guys, lots of dates and lots of parties. Then she went away to Queens and I went to Western. I was really surprised when she came back to Mariposa."

"Why do you say that?"

"What did this small town hold for her? When she went away, it was her chance to stay away. She always said that when she left it would be forever. Cathy couldn't stand Mariposa. It was too small for her."

"Why did she come back then?"

"She couldn't get a job in her field. When a job opened up at the library, she decided to take it temporarily until something better came along. She told me she was just biding her time."

"Had she changed when she came back?"

Clara shrugged. "She was different. It was nice to have her back. I had started teaching school and it was great to see her again, but it wasn't the same. Cathy had changed. On the surface she was quieter. But I felt she was restless, adrift, somehow distracted, not focused."

"When was the last time you saw her?"

"We were supposed to meet Friday at Brewery Bay for a TGIF celebration. You know, I understand James was going to meet her also, but she stood him up. James was acting a bit hyper that evening. I couldn't believe the news when I heard it today," said Clara biting her lip.

David waited for her to gain control, then he said, "Who else was there that evening at the Brewery Bay in your group?"

"I mentioned James. Bob Thompson was there. He teaches with me at Mariposa High and Tom, Tom Ball whose father owns Ball Haberdashery on Mississauga, and Ted Chirp. We were just sitting around drinking light beer and spritzers, nothing heavy."

David smiled at her school marm attempt to protect her reputation in a small town.

"Was there any man that Cathy was strongly interested in?" asked David.

Clara shook her head. "I don't think Cathy was really interested in any of the guys. She would go out with them for a while. Then pick a fight. Break up with them. That was her pattern."

"Let's go back to James, Clara. Can you tell me about that friendship?"

Clara shrugged her shoulders. "Cathy liked him. But I don't think he would do it. He wouldn't harm a fly. Did you get a chance to see how his mother orders him around? He's completely under her thumb. Cathy liked him as a friend, but that was all. I don't think it was much more than that."

"What was Cathy's relationship to Bob Thompson?"

"Oh they went out a few times, several months ago, but I don't think too much came of it. They were still friendly."

"How about Tom Ball?" David saw her falter, saw a slight flush creep up her neck to her face

"Oh, Tom," said Clara trying to appear off hand, "she wasn't close to him at all. She went out with him a few times back in September. I don't think it was serious."

Clara's flushed face turned quickly away from him, but not before he caught her discomfort. Ah, there's more to this than meets the eye.

"Can you recall anything she said about him?" said David, his ears perking up. "Did she find him attractive?"

Again Clara blushed. "She said he was a good catch. His father has inherited wealth. Yes, I guess she set her sights on Tom Ball. I guess we all have." She corrected herself, "Every girl has."

"Were you interested in him?"

"Just as a friend."

Liar, thought David.

"How long have you known Tom Ball?"

"All my life," said Clara. "He lives next door to me. His house is that large one on the edge of the hill with the tennis courts and the pool. As a child, I learned to play tennis on those courts. I spent many idyllic summer days swimming and playing tennis with Tom. Then Tom went away to Ridley College in St. Catherines. I didn't see him that much. When he came home on vacation, he ran with a wild crowd. Cathy was one of that crowd. Later I went to Western and so did Tom to get his B.A. in business administration, but our paths rarely crossed."

"Were Cathy and Tom ever lovers?"

"She was a friend of his," said Clara firmly, "they were not lovers."

"Are you sure?" asked David peering into those big brown eyes.

"Why don't you ask Tom? I've got to go," said Clara abruptly. "It's late. I've got to go."

"Of course," said David. "I want to get in touch with you at a later date. Is that fine with you?"

"Of course."

"Can I give you a lift?"

"Thanks just the same. But I have my car parked outside."

Damn, thought David, watching her leave. Why did she have to have a car? Going to keep my eye on that one. Where there's smoke, there's fire. He sighed. David, you fool, you're attracted to this school marm. Don't let your attraction interfere with your objectivity.

Chapter 6

It was Tuesday. And Dr. Frost had said he would have the autopsy report ready in about four days. David decided to phone him to ask how it was coming along.

Dr Frost's voice was bland and urbane. "I was just about to call you. The Snifton girl was strangled. Signs of strangulation show that, besides the plum coloured band encircling her neck, there were pin-point haemorrhages from burst capillaries in the whites of her eyes and bruises to the windpipe above the band on her neck. The hyoid bone had been broken. She'd been strangled with a cloth. We found red mohair fibres imbedded in the skin of her neck. Probably, that mohair scarf of hers found beside the body on the ice was what was used to kill her. Forensic tests will confirm it."

"Can you tell me, doctor, what amount of strength would it take to do it?"

"It wouldn't take much strength. There wasn't any sign of a struggle. The victim may have been caught by surprise. That is something you will have to determine. There were no self-defence wounds or marks on her hands or her arms. There was no bruising elsewhere."

"Was it done by a man or a woman?"

"Either. It doesn't take much pressure to snap the hyoid bone."

"Can you tell me, doctor, the exact time of death?"

"The most accurate test depends on body temperature which involves the leaching of potassium into the vitreous humour."

David sighed. Here comes another long winded biology lecture from Dr. Frost. He will practice his speech for the inquest. He closed his eyes as Dr. Frost droned on.

"The cells of a living person are high in sodium, low in potassium. When death occurs, the cells break down and are stored in the surrounding environment. Potassium leaches into the vitreous humour at a rate of one milli/mol per hour. In the vitreous humour, there was found to be ten milli/mols of potassium. The body was found at ten a.m. Interesting, huh? That bit about the potassium? So taking this as a benchmark, it would have to be around midnight."

More than I ever need to know, thought David. "Was she raped before being strangled?"

"No, there are no signs that she had been sexually assaulted. There are no traces of semen in the vagina or anus. No disturbance of the clothing. Her underwear was intact."

"Any signs of drugs? Pot? Cocaine in the blood?"

"None."

"But here's something interesting. As a healthy young female, she had already one abortion and at the time of her death, she was three months pregnant."

David whistled. "That gives me something to go on."

"Yes, I thought you'd like that."

So the sweet, young librarian goody two shoes was three months pregnant. Now I have got to find out who the father was. Maybe her murderer.

Chapter 7

The sky was clear with only light flurries. It looked like a fairly nice winter's day. Greg was bent over his desk, writing up his reports of a couple of break and enters and loveable Clancy delivered the good news as soon as David arrived.

"Bob White called. He still can't get here. There have been so many problems over at Barrie. A homicide and a suicide have just come up. The homicide began as a suicide case, and the suicide began as a homicide. He asked that you carry on. By the way, how are things going?"

"Slowly. Going to interview a former boyfriend, a hot suspect at the moment. Any calls while I was out?"

"Why?" grinned Clancy, "would anyone want to call you? Just kidding. A word of caution. Keep the net wide open, Davy. You don't want to have a fixed idea on who murdered somebody. You don't want to show tunnel vision. If you do, on the stand during the trial the defence lawyers can tear that evidence to shreds, in that you didn't consider other possibilities. Keep it wide open."

There were a lot of questions that David had to find the answers to. Why would Cathy go to such an isolated spot? She must have been meeting someone. Otherwise I don't see why she was there, late at night, after the park's rink had shut down. Someone had arranged to meet her there. Who was that someone and when had they called her? At work? It must be at work where she took all her calls. But who?

David checked for his phone messages. Nothing that couldn't wait. His number one suspect, so far, was Tom Ball.

Ball's Men's Haberdashery on Mississauga Street created the successful illusion that it was just a family style house set in the country that doubled as a store while outside the deer and the moose roamed. When David entered, a three tone chime sounded. To one side of the room a large brown leather sofa and chair had been placed in front of a log fireplace. On the opposite side of the room, leather bound books sat on shelves. Were they real or were they fake? Dried sunflowers stood in an umbrella stand by the door. A china chamber pot, a centrepiece and a brass spittoon, to be looked at but not used, said money, money, money.

David hated to admit that he liked to look at their stuff and he did buy the odd thing. But the Paisley silk ties, the Polo lounge cashmere sweaters, the St. Laurent silk shirts were far too rich for his wallet. He glanced at the hand knitted Norwegian ski sweaters $500.00 a pop. In the centre of the room, a pile of flyers on a table announced a twenty-five percent discount. Maybe he would be able to pick up something after all.

The overpowering smell of cinnamon coming from a pot pourri bowl hit his nostrils, "Kerchoo. Kerchoo." He couldn't control himself. "Kerchoo."

"Can I help you?"

Embarrassed he looked into the tanned face of Tom Ball, which emanated good health. His teeth were pepsodent white. In his open v-neck cashmere sweater, red and white checked Ralph Lauren shirt, lounge trousers and Bass penny loafers, Tom Ball had Ivy League written all over him. David had never taken to Tom, and a prickle of irritation travelled up his spine.

"I'm here on business, Tom," said David stiffly. "I want to ask you about Cathy Snifton."

"Are you sure there's nothing I can show you before we talk?" said Tom picking up a navy blue cashmere scarf.

'Quite sure," said David grimly.

"Well in that case, can we talk outside of here? My father has a heart condition and I really don't think... I don't want my father to get excited and overly concerned. How about coffee at Apple Annie's?"

David nodded.

They found a quiet table at the back of the restaurant.

Sitting across from Tom, studying his features, David reckoned that God had been too kind in giving Tom dimples in his cheeks and a cleft in his chin. But he was also pleased to notice that a small birth mark, diamond shaped was etched under his left eye and that his eyes were just a centimetre too close to the bridge of his nose. He was not Mr. Perfect.

"Tell me about Cathy and what she meant to you."

Tom paused and flexed his knuckles in front of him on

the table until they were white. "Cathy was a nice girl. I'm very sorry to hear what had happened to her. Very sorry."

"Did you know her well?"

"You mean, did I go out with her? Yeah, I went out with her a few times."

"A few times! Come again, Mr. Ball," snapped David.

"Yeah, I went out with her. Notice I am using the past tense."

"How far back does the past tense go?"

"Look, I want to co-operate with you. Don't give me a hard time," said Tom, flashing his I'm-a-nice guy grin. "I hung around her in high school. It wasn't serious. I made no promises. Hey man, that's a long time ago. She came back to Mariposa and wanted to take up where we left off. I didn't. I couldn't see myself getting seriously involved with Cathy. Right from the beginning, I made it clear to her I wasn't looking for a wife. Her response was that she wasn't looking for a husband."

"Where did you go on dates?"

"Around. Strictly casual. Drives in the country, eating at take out places, little restaurants and bars. No big deal, no red roses and candy, just beer and pizza. You get the picture."

"Yeah." said David, "but not picture perfect."

"Cathy didn't complain."

"Were you sexually active with Cathy?" Of course he was. Maybe he'd try to deny it. David tensed waiting for his answer.

A chair scraped on the floor behind them. David could hear the conversation at another table. A man was asking his wife for the car keys. He could smell the coffee and the muffins and hear the clatter of dishes being scraped and stacked for the dishwasher, but he kept his eyes fixed on Tom's face.

"Okay, okay," said Tom, throwing up his hands. "I wasn't the first one or the only one. Cathy wasn't a virgin when I met her. There were people before me and after me."

"Was she an easy fuck?" asked David, sarcastically, surprised by the heat of his own words. He wanted to smash that conceited, self-satisfied look off Tom's face.

"It wasn't like that at all," said Tom defensively. "I liked Cathy, but I didn't love her. She wanted and needed so much from me emotionally and I couldn't give it to her. Our relationship spun out of control. She wanted a serious commitment. I told her that I wasn't ready to settle down."

"When was that?"

"A couple of months ago, maybe three months ago."

"Really? What brought this 'serious talk' on?"

"It was always there. I just had to tell her flat out. I didn't want to string her along any more, promises of something more when I couldn't offer her what she wanted."

"Did you murder her?"

"Why should I want to murder her?"

"To get rid of her, to get her off your case."

"You got me all wrong. Cathy went out with quite a few people."

"Not according to her mother. Name some."

"Her mother," snorted Tom, "What did she know. All her mother worried about was where her next meal was coming from, so that she could continue to sit in her favourite chair watching TV. Her mother never cared about Cathy, except to ask her to get this and that. Cathy was just a servant. Cathy had to look elsewhere for the love she craved. I will co-operate in any way. But you're not going to pin this murder on me."

"Let's go over last Friday night. After you left work, what did you do?"

"Easy. I joined the gang down at Brewery Bay to have a drink."

"Was Cathy there?"

"No. I didn't see any sign of her. She's usually there. But then sometimes she doesn't show." Tom shrugged. "I thought that I would just say hello in the Happy Hour after work as usual. With Cathy," he paused, to emphasize his words, "I intended to keep it light and nothing more. Say hello and then go home and feed my dog. When I got home, my dog was restless. He'd been shut in all day."

"Your dog was restless. Please spare me. Now you're going to tell me you decided to be kind to your dog and take him for a walk. Am I going to believe this? We have you, Tom, a healthy young male, walking his dog on a Friday night for exercise. Come on. I'm not Santa Clause. You're not Dick and your dog isn't called Spot."

"Obviously, you've never owned a dog. I put a leash on Tag and took him out for a run through the park."

"What time was this? Did you see anyone in the park who can verify your presence there with your dog?"

"Around ten p.m. The music was still on. The park was deserted almost. I didn't see anyone and just came home."

"So your alibi for the time that the murder was committed is your dog," said David sarcastically. "I'm sure you can do better than that. We'll be in touch. Think over that last evening and see if you can't come up with something better. It sounds pathetic, your dog story." David rose to his feet and stomped out.

If Tom Ball was walking with his dog, and he wanted to meet up with Cathy, he would have had to first take the dog home. I can't see him strangling her with the dog present—the dog would be making a hell of a racket. Someone would have heard it. He would first have had to take the dog home, then come back to the park to meet up with Cathy. It's possible but not probable. It's a bit of a stretch. Also there would have to be enough time to do it, if it were premeditated. I think according to reports that this was a sudden attack, perhaps a surprise attack and she must have known her attacker because there were no defensive wounds or bruising on the arms or hands. There was no attempt to fend off the attacker.

Chapter 8

With the autopsy report finalized, the coroner could release the body to the family. Friday was the chosen day of Cathy Snifton's funeral. The forecast was grim, overcast with snow flurries. Clancy suggested that he take in the funeral to check out the mourners. Some murderers liked to attend their victim's funeral or grave. They got a charge out of it for some morbid reason.

"Attending will be difficult," said Clancy, "bring your hankie."

The funeral was scheduled for two p.m.

David made a note to question Mrs. Snifton again, but not today, today was not appropriate.

He had heard the gossip around town. Mrs. Snifton had stipulated that she wanted a small, inexpensive funeral, a short service at Miller's Funeral Home followed by interment in Mariposa Cemetery. Reverend Day and the choir at Mariposa United had offered to have it in the church, and to donate their services but Mrs. Snifton was firm. She didn't feel comfortable holding the funeral in a church. That was easy to figure out, the gossips said, she hadn't darkened the church door in years.

Miller's Funeral Home was a large red brick Victorian house with gables and gingerbread trim. Its roof had many chimneys. When it had been converted into a funeral home, the front door and vestibule area had been widened to accommodate pallbearers carrying a coffin. A circular driveway replaced the solitary side walk. The large living room and the parlour on either side of the front door now served as individual chapels, with folding doors connecting to extended rooms.

To make sure that he was one of the first to arrive, David got there early. He read the black velvet covered notice board posted in the doorway with white plastic letters that read, *'Chapel 1. Cathy Snifton. 2 p.m.'*

At the door greeting mourners, stood the cheerless Mr. Miller in a black dinner suit, extending a cold hand. He indicated to David to sign the Sympathy book on a lectern. David made a mental note to ask Miller for a Xerox copy of all the mourners' names after the service. At the graveside ceremony he would have to rely on his own memory and TV footage taken by the Barrie TV station.

David walked down the deep, purple plush aisle carpet, past the empty pews and then crossed in front of the altar. Bouquets of chrysanthemums, gladioli and white carnations flanked the altar. In a curtained-off area to the side of the room, banked by heavy blue drapes, was the open, plain pine coffin resting on a raised catafalque containing the remains of Cathy Snifton.

The smell of sweet flowers, mixed in with dead flesh, was nauseating. He coughed to clear his throat and willed himself to look down. It was less than a year since he had stood in this same spot looking down at his dead wife and their infant son.

Cathy's long flowing Botticelli-like auburn hair was now held in place by two pearl barrettes. At her neck a black velvet band with a large cameo broach hid the burn marks caused by the strangulation. A cosmetician had dusted some powder on her freckled cheeks and added a dash of lipstick to those cold lips.

At the bottom of the casket, a large spray of white roses rested. David leaned over to read the signature on the embossed white card. 'I will love you, forever, Mother.'

He cleared his throat again, then walked around to the other bouquets, examining the cards. There were names of couples, with 'Love from Helen and Harry', 'Sue and Sam,' 'Terry and George.' An attractive small bouquet of rosebuds caught his eye. The card read, 'With love, James'. There were no other cards from men. Cathy's admirers, whomever they were, had been discreet.

A white gowned Reverend Day strode in, shook hands quickly with David and then headed to the office of the Funeral Director. Several old ladies, whispering with heads bowed, slipped into a back pew. A mixed group of young and old faces, probably from the Mariposa United Church Choir, came in and sat down three rows from the front. Mrs. Sandy slipped in several rows ahead of him. A pale, hatless Mabel Day sat down beside her.

The last to arrive was Mrs. Snifton. The sobbing was so loud that David shifted around to stare.

Mrs. Snifton, a fat waddling figure in a tatty black lace dress which reached to her ankles, hobbled down the main aisle. On her swollen feet were her bedroom slippers.

Howling in pain, she cried, "I can't face this. I can't face this."

Somebody do something, thought David.

Thankfully Mrs. Sandy stepped out into the aisle and took Mrs. Snifton by the arm. She led her to the front pew and sat down with her.

Composed, but pale, Reverend Day stepped out from behind a curtain and onto the dais in front of them.

"I bring you words of comfort. As friends and loved ones of Cathy we are hurt and angered by what has happened to her. We want to ask God why? Why was this lovely young woman taken from us? We ask ourselves, why did God allow this to happen? Why should Cathy Snifton, a good person be taken from us? There are no answers. I can only give you words of comfort by reading from Psalm 23: Verse 1-6. The Lord is My Shepherd. I shall not want...."

David's ears picked up the slight tremor in his voice, but abruptly his concentration was broken. A warm hand had fallen on his thigh. It was Mira. Didn't she have any respect for the occasion? He pushed her hand away.

"Misery needs company," whispered Mira.

The service was finally over. Mr. Miller beckoned for Mrs. Snifton to follow him for a last viewing of the deceased, as the drapes swung around to close off the view of the casket.

Like the others he waited while Mrs. Snifton struggled to her feet with her cane. With a gigantic effort, she hobbled over to the side. David could hear the voice of Mr. Miller saying softly but firmly, "We have to close the casket, Mrs. Snifton." But Mrs. Snifton cried out, protesting, "No, no, no," and then scuffling sounds, followed by, "There, there. We must pull ourselves together," followed by the gently sobbing of Mrs. Snifton.

Outside the funeral home, Mrs. Snifton was helped down the steps to the lead car by Reverend Day.

Mira whispered, "Why don't we take my car to drive to

the cemetery and then I can drop you off back here? There's no point in taking two cars."

It was nice and warm sitting in Mira's car. Mira for once concentrated on her driving and David didn't have to keep up polite conversation.

The snow had begun to fall again. Soft, light flakes settled down on the windshield. The skeletal branches of the trees were black against the greyness of the sky. When they finally arrived at the cemetery gates, the wind had picked up. Make the graveside service quick, prayed David, or we'll freeze to death. But, more to the point, he didn't want to be reminded that his wife was buried here also.

At the gravesite, with the canvas canopy flapping around in the wind, Reverend Day sprinkled a handful of earth onto the casket, intoning, "Ashes to ashes, dust to dust." Mrs. Snifton, oblivious to all fell on her knees and placed her lined tear-stained cheek against the side of the coffin, crying out in despair, "Cathy, Cathy what am I going to do without you?"

The other mourners, in embarrassment, avoided looking at her. Mr. Miller reached over and pulled Mrs. Snifton to her feet. Reverend Day took her other elbow. "God will help us face this, Mrs. Snifton. We are not alone. We live in God's world." Then, half dragging, half supporting her heavy body, they propelled her back to the car. David watched them go.

"Come on, it's over. Over." Mira pulled him by the elbow. "No lingering afterthoughts. Let's go. A better idea, let's take the rest of the afternoon off and go back to my place for a drink." David smiled. Yes, he thought, the best cure for a depressing funeral is to hop into the sack immediately afterwards.

"Unless," she raised her eyebrows tauntingly at him, "you'd rather work?"

Obediently, David followed Mira back to her car and they followed the other cars out of the cemetery. It was snowing again. David gave a last look back. He could make out the grave diggers, like dark shadows of untouchables, emerge from behind the surrounding bushes with their spades and lanterns, and softly shovel the black earth into the grave.

"It's not wise to look back," said Mira catching his glance. She drove silently, concentrating on the road. The snow was making the going tough. Mira turned down a street and parked her car in the driveway of a semi-detached, frame house.

"Let's lighten up, shall we?" said Mira getting out her key. Inside, the hall was in darkness. Mira groped along the wall for the light switch before picking up the post on the mat.

"Let's get the coats off. Make yourself comfortable." She indicated a leopard-skin covered sofa. With the toe of her boot, she straightened out the white shag rug underneath the glass and chrome coffee table.

David sat down. Mira gestured at the walls. "When I was married, I used to have all the walls painted white. The room looked all white and very nice. Now I prefer warm, strong colours like yellow. It's more cheerful. Whew, it's cold in here," said Mira, rubbing her hands together. "I'll turn on the heater in the fireplace. Now, let's see about a drink."

In one corner of the room, David noticed a small bar with two tall chrome and leather bar stools. Behind the bar were several shelves and bottles of liquor.

There was a tall Dieffenbachia with stringy leaves. It needs water, he thought. His wife had loved plants. Mira followed his gaze.

"A Dieffenbachia is very delicate, just like me. I know what you are thinking," she said defensively, "This plant needs low light, no drafts and lots of watering. I've got a job and can't spend all my time looking after it. Besides the dry heat in this place in the evenings when I come home is killing off everything I have. I should have cactus plants in here. Enough of plants. How about some brandy to lift our spirits?"

"That will be fine, Mira. Don't go to too much trouble."

"Nothing is too much trouble for you, David," said Mira coquettishly.

David laughed.

Mira handed him a heavy tumbler. She clicked her glass against his and huskily whispered, "Here's to us."

David let the brandy float back in his throat and felt the burn. "Cheers, Mira."

"Well?" said Mira, settling back into the sofa, "how's the investigation going? Do you think I just brought you up here for your body?"

David's face reddened. That's exactly what he thought.

"The case so far, Mira, to keep our conversation on a higher level, is that I believe Cathy knew who killed her. Cathy must have been very confident to walk out to that isolated spot with someone she trusted. I don't think Cathy thought going there was unusual. She knew the park well from skating there. Why did she go there? Whom did she meet? How long in advance was the arrangement made? A few hours before? A few days before? An hour? Was she to meet someone and a third person followed her to that spot? That is a possibility. The main point is that she was killed there, not elsewhere. What I want to find out is if she told anyone that she was going there. Cathy was three months pregnant at the time of her death. Any ideas who might be the father? Was she going to meet her lover, the father of her child?"

Myra whistled. "My, my, the horny librarian gets pregnant! Her lover silences her so that his reputation won't be ruined and he won't have to marry her. Aw come on! That script is too Victorian for words. Not in this day and age."

"Who were Cathy's lovers?"

"Search me. The rumours around town were that Cathy was a hot one. I heard that she went out with Tom Ball before she went away to university. She had a fling with him and then when she came back, tried to pick up where she left off." Mira pursed her lips. "He's one of the first people to talk to, but that would be too easy." She wrinkled her nose, "The obvious suspect isn't always the right person."

"Thanks Mira. that gives me something to go on. I've already interviewed him once, but I'm sure he has more to tell us. But was he the only one?"

"Oh, knock it off. The chase doesn't have to start at this very moment. Let's just relax," said Mira softly and she brushed her face against his, touching his cheek, his nose and then his lips.

David smelled her perfume. He felt the heat of her breasts and the warmth of her breath upon his face. He felt hot flames lick his groin. Things were going too fast. He had to say something before things got out of hand.

"Mira, I have something that must be said. Since my wife

died, I've been dead inside. I'm not ready for a relationship, let alone a commitment."

"Let me be the judge of that," murmured Mira, biting his ear. "Close your eyes," she commanded.

David sank back against the large sofa cushions as Mira's experienced fingers pushed and probed. His tie was the first to go. Then his shirt, his belt. Mira's soft breast pressed against his bare skin. Her hand was on his bulging groin, rubbing gently. David felt his heart racing. His member had a will of its own. Mira's head bent down, as she first kissed his lips, his neck and then his member.

As each sensation came closer and closer together, David sank, swirling, and tumbling, until his brain burst in a shower of stars.

When he awoke, he heard Mira in the kitchen making coffee. She poked her head around the corner, "Refreshed?" she asked. "Tender loving care is what we both needed."

"No argument there, Mira. But I have to go. Thanks for everything. But now I have to work on a murder investigation."

"Who's holding you back," grinned Mira. "Keep in touch"

*****

An hour later, when he was back at his desk, trying to get caught up with his paper work, he heard someone in the outer office asking Clancy where he was.

"Go right down the hall, Madam. He's that lonely guy sitting by the radiator."

Thanks a lot, Clancy. How flattering! He looked up to see Mildred Lemon standing meekly in front of him, holding a string bag.

"Good to see you again, Mildred. What can I do for you?"

"I've come on my lunch hour. I, uh, would appreciate it if you wouldn't mention my visit to my boss, Mrs. Proudfoot. You know how she is." David caught her eyes, those washed out, pale, watery eyes, before she glanced down at her feet. "She would make my life unbearable."

"What is it?" asked David, encouragingly.

"I remembered something. I was so upset that I'd

forgotten all about it. But you asked me to remember all that happened that day. There was another caller that afternoon, before Cathy left work. But the call was very short and I heard her say, 'It's none of your business. Stay out of my life." That's all I can tell you. I hope it will help. Cathy was kind to me and I want her killer caught. I don't know whether it's important or not."

"Everything is important," said David. "Thank you for telling me."

*****

The sky was clear with only light flurries. It looked like a fairly nice winter day. At the office, Greg was bent over his desk, writing up his reports of a couple of break and enters and loveable Clancy delivered the good news as soon as David arrived.

"Bob White called. He still can't get here. There have been so many problems over at Barrie. He asked that you carry on. By the way, how are things going?"

"Slowly. Going to interview a former boyfriend, a hot suspect at the moment. Any calls while I was out?"

"Why" grinned Clancy, "would anyone want to call you? Just kidding. A word of caution. Keep the net wide open, Davy. You don't want to have a fixed idea on who murdered somebody. You don't want to show tunnel vision. If you do, on the stand during the trial, defence lawyers can tear that evidence to shreds, because you didn't consider other possibilities. Keep it wide open."

There were a lot of questions that David had to find the answers to. Why would Cathy go out to such an isolated spot? She must have been meeting someone, someone who wanted to talk to her and then surprised her by strangling her. Otherwise I don't see why she was there, late at night, after the park's rink had shut down? Someone had called her to meet her there. Who was that someone and when had they called her? At work? It must be at work where she took all her calls. But who?

Chapter 9

David figured he needed another chat with Tom Ball to see if he could get more details. The devil is in the details.

He phoned Ball Haberdashery and asked to speak to Tom. "I need to speak to you again. I need your help in fleshing out some details."

"Okay, I have a break coming up. Meet you across the street at Apple Annie's."

Tom was sitting at a back table, with a cup of black coffee. "Why do you want to see me again?"

"Well Tom, you're in the picture, you were in the park before she was killed."

"I had nothing to do with it. Will I need to have a lawyer present the next time I speak to you?"

"No, just answer the questions. Cathy was three months pregnant when she was murdered. Was she blackmailing you? Was she asking you for money for an abortion?"

"She wasn't pregnant by me," replied Tom with clenched teeth. "I practiced safe sex. You'll have to look elsewhere."

"Did she ask you for money?"

"Keep your voice down, I don't want people to hear."

"Was she also trying to pressure you into marriage?"

"She tried to, but it didn't work."

"That's a good motive to murder someone. Any ideas who the father might be?"

"Cathy was hot blooded. It could have been anyone. Who knows? I never kept track of whom she hung around with. It was none of my business. She was her own person."

"Let's go over your statement again about walking your dog that night in the park. You claim you didn't see anyone in particular. You just went for a walk with the dog and then came home and went to bed."

"Well, I did see two people that I knew but I didn't think they would have any bearing on the case."

"Let me be the judge of that."

"Around ten p.m. I did bump into two people but I think they would be too embarrassed to come forward."

"Will you clarify that remark?"

73

"It was like this. My dog started to paw and bark at a man getting out of his car. I went over to see what the fuss was about. It was Neary, the church organist for Mariposa United, and he appeared flustered. Tag jumped up and put his paws on his trousers. He was just being friendly. Neary wasn't too happy. He yelled, 'Can't you keep that damn dog of yours under control?' It was then that I noticed Neary's fly was open.

"There was a movement in the car. Another man looked out through the open door. I didn't pay much attention to him because Neary was shouting and threatening to call the dog pound and tell them that I had a dangerous animal on the loose. I yelled back at him. It was obvious what they had been doing. I asked them why they didn't do this in the privacy of their own home rather than here in a public park. I considered myself broadminded, but to be humping some guy in the dead of winter in a car in a public park, yuk! What a creep!"

"What time did this occur?"

"Before ten p.m. I could tell because the music was still on."

"You mean you don't wear a watch."

"I wear a watch but I didn't bother with the time. It wasn't important."

"Tom," said David. leaning closer, "I think you recognized the other man in the car. I'm right aren't I? Who was he?"

"Yeah, I hate to get him involved in this. He is just a nice, harmless, quiet guy who wouldn't hurt a fly. You may have seen him around. It's James. I wish it wasn't but it was."

David made a mental note. That takes care of Neary and James Muir.

"What did they do after they met you? Where did they go?"

"They headed out of the park in the direction where James lives. Neary was quite angry."

"Did you see anyone else? Did you recognize anyone at all? Was there a man or woman on their own?"

Tom bit his lip. "I don't think so. On the way back I went by Clara's house. But then I was so tired that I went home to bed."

"What time did you get home?"

"Around eleven thirty."

"Did you see anyone on the street?"

"I can't recall seeing anyone," Tom gave a nervous smile, "The only one that can vouch for me is my dog."

David had a desperate urge to reach across the table and grab him by the throat, but instead he banged the pepper shaker down on the table.

"I want to know the exact streets that you went down."

"I walked through the park, over the railroad tracks and then went up the hill on Brant Avenue, past Clara's house. It was too late to say 'hi' and I continued walking further up the hill."

"You didn't by chance see anybody?"

"The streets were deserted."

David got up and threw some change down on the table. "It's an insult to my intelligence, Tom, to listen any more to this garbage you're telling me. Do you think I'm going to sit here and swallow this dog story? Think again."

David stalked out of the door. What a load of bull, and that conceited ape thinks that I am going to swallow it. A dumb cop, well he can think again.

Chapter 10

Clancy looked up from his desk. "Did Old Man Winter give you frostbite? Your red nose looks like it is going to fall off. Don't let all that snow on your coat fall on me when you shake it off. I'm cold enough these days. It must be minus twenty outside. Before you sit down, turn the thermostat up."

Clancy was like a mother hen, always keeping an eye on him and telling him what to do. But he had to grin and bear it. Clancy was his senior officer and there wasn't a thing he could do about it. This was his first murder case and he was just feeling his way.

"Another thing, Davy, Rome wasn't built in a day."

That was true.

"A suggestion only, Davy. I am not telling you what to do. You're a big boy now. It might be a good idea to check out anyone that is on probation for violent assault or for violent offences in the area. Also, get the names of men who have a rap sheet for physical assault and battery, cons who have done time." said Clancy, "One of them might be a repeat offender and our murderer. It's a lot of boring slogging. But that's what it takes to prepare a case for the crown, eliminating all the possibilities, and not keeping your focus too tight at the beginning."

"Thanks."

"You're welcome."

So David sat down at the computer and scrolled down through the list looking for possibilities. There were at least four men up for domestic assault in the past three years. Should he interview everyone on the off chance that they were in the park on the thirteenth? It was a good start. He wrote down their names, Kevin Bracken, Steven Jones, Rick Miller. Ted Chirp was the most recent entry. All had battery and assault charges against them for attacking their wife, girlfriend or neighbour. Most incidents involved alcohol. Kevin Bracken had smacked his girlfriend after an evening of drinking. Steven Jones had gotten into a fight down at Brewery Bay and had smashed a glass, threatening the owner. Rick Miller had gotten into a drunken brawl down at the harbour after an evening of drinking. Ted Chirp was arrested twice for assaulting his wife.

He began phoning them. Kevin Bracken was the first person he called. It was lunch hour so he might be home. He was.

"Just getting my lunch on. What's this about?"

David identified himself. "A few questions. Investigating the murder of a young woman. Cathy Snifton."

Yeah, I heard about that. Sad. But I had nothing to do with it. You can't pin it on me."

"Where were you on Friday, the thirteenth?

"Minding my own business. No, I was, let me see Friday, the thirteenth you say. Yeah, I remember I was out on a date with a new girlfriend. We went to the movies."

"What was the name of the movie?"

"The Avengers. It was quite long."

"What did you do afterwards?"

"Do you want all the fine details?"

"Yes."

"We went back to her house and went to bed. She's my alibi."

"Can you give me the phone number of your girlfriend so I can eliminate you from my list of suspects?"

"Sure. No problem. Helga Smith. She's a nurse. She's doing shifts at Mariposa General. We were together the whole evening and afterwards at her house."

Of course, David thought the girlfriend will vouch for him. He put her name down on his list to call.

Steven Jones was not at home but his answering machine said he was at work down at the Knock Wood Furniture store and to contact him there. David decided to drop in for a brief chat later.

Rick Miller was the next one on his list. He was at home, laid off from his job at the lumber mill. Where was he on the thirteenth? Well he certainly wasn't down at Brewery Bay, that was for sure. The manager had told him not to come back. I was in the Dead Tired pool room shooting pool."

"Any witnesses?"

"Just the guys around me."

"Name one."

"Larry Smith."

"Where can I get hold of him?"

"You can find him at the pool hall most days. He's on disability."

"Thanks. Will do."

"What's this about anyway?"

"A girl was murdered, Cathy Snifton."

"Oh, her. I read something about that in the papers. What a shame. I was at the pool hall until it closed."

The next name was Ted Chirp, twice up for assaulting his wife in the past two years. He gave him a call at Real Deal real estate office on Mississauga. He introduced himself and the reason why he called. Where was he on the night of the thirteenth?

"I was here at my office selling real estate until around five or six, then I went over to Brewery Bay for Happy Hour. I was there for a couple of hours then I went home."

"Is that your local?"

"Yes, the price of beer is reasonable and there's nice company. Sometimes I get lucky."

"Did you know Cathy Snifton? She used to go there on Friday nights."

"I knew of her, I knew her by sight. Why?"

"That's all, just by sight?"

"Everything was pretty casual there, a drop-in after work on Friday evenings."

"So you were there all evening."

"Yes, I went home later, alone," Mm, thought David, this one is a possibility. He probably dated her and does not want to admit it. Where there's smoke there's fire. He made a mental note to drop into Brewery Bay, during the next Friday's Happy Hour.

There was a lot of ground to cover. He went down another list of those in the area who had spent time incarcerated.

He came to one name, connected to a serious charge of

manslaughter. Kerr served ten years, with time off for good behavior, for killing his wife. One night he had strangled her in a drunken rage. In the bedroom the wife had nagged him, insulted his masculinity, ridiculed him, until he snapped. After serving his sentence he was put on probation for the rest of his life. Place of work was listed as Mariposa United, in a custodial capacity.

Mariposa United. What a coincidence. Cathy's church. This person I should definitely go and interview. Cathy's murder may have been by a random attack, an attack based on opportunity, being at the wrong place at the wrong time. But to get her to that isolated spot, it must have been someone she knew and trusted.

He put on his jacket and headed out. He found the side door to the church open and let himself in. The church was in darkness. He walked down the hall, calling out, "Hello, hello, anybody here?" Ahead of him was the church office. He opened the door and went in. Miss Cassidy got up from her desk. "How can I help you?"

"I'm here to see George Kerr."

"Is there a problem?" Miss Cassidy couldn't hide her curiosity. She couldn't remember the last time that the OPP had made a call at the church.

"None, but I will need his help."

"I will ring for him. He is probably vacuuming the ladies' parlour. We had a meeting last night after which we served coffee and treats."

A tall, thin man in T-shirt, jeans and running shoes, appeared in the doorway. He appeared to be in his early forties. When he saw David's uniform, he looked physically shaken.

"My name is David Scott. Can we sit somewhere so that I can ask you a few questions?"

"We can go down to the ladies' parlour. There are some chairs there. What do you want from me? I've done my time and I want to keep my job. It's hard for a middle aged male to get a job, any job, and I don't want mine to be jeopardized. I lost my last job because my employer got wind of what I'd done. I'm trying to go straight."

"I'm going to ask you just a few questions, that's all. Where were you on Friday the thirteenth of December between the hours of ten p.m. and one am? "David took out his notebook to write down Kerr's answers.

"Is this in connection with the girl that got murdered?"

"Yes."

"Let me think. I lock up here around five pm. on Fridays. The church is usually busy on the weekends for weddings and services. I came in early to turn the heat on. I headed home. Maybe I stopped for a coffee at Apple Annie's, which I sometimes do. I like the atmosphere there, cheerful and then I might have picked up something to eat from the Mariposa Market. I don't have a big appetite. As usual I went to my rooming house and went to bed."

"That's it? No one can vouch for you after ten pm?"

"I was in bed. Alone."

"I see." David wrote down his answer. "Cathy Snifton, sang in the church choir here. Did you see her around the building at all? Bump into her? Have a conversation with her that week or in the previous weeks?"

"I knew who she was, but I didn't have any connection with her, never spoke to her."

"Are you sure?"

"I don't know her, only the sight of her, never had a conversation with her."

"We'll be in touch," said David putting away his notebook and getting up.

"You believe me don't you? I had nothing to do with her murder. I will not have this pinned on me."

"It's early yet in our investigation. Can anyone vouch for your movements that evening like a friend, or someone where you live?"

"I minded my own business and just went home. I didn't see anybody that I recall. It was last week. I can't remember everybody."

David wondered, what would George's motive be for murder? He would have to dig deeper to find a connection, but he seemed genuine enough, unless proven otherwise.

Chapter 11

He now had to do a little housecleaning to check out the alibis. First on his list, Helga Smith, the nurse. He phoned Mariposa General to see if he could get her. *'Paging Helga Smith, Paging Helga Smith.'*

She came to the phone. "I hope this call is important, because I am not supposed to take personal calls at work."

David identified himself and gave her the preliminaries. "I need some information. Can you verify Kevin Bracken was with you all evening on Friday, December the thirteenth?"

"Give me a minute. Yes he was. We went to a movie and then back to my house where he stayed the night."

"Do you recall the name of the movie?"

"The Avengers. Yes that's it. What's this all about? Is Kevin a suspect?"

"No, he's got an alibi, you. Thanks for your help." He hung up.

Next, a short saunter down to theDead Tired Pool Hall, located on a narrow alley behind the RBC building. He was always amazed to see perfectly fit men playing pool in the afternoon in the darkened room. Some were seniors, some were on disability, but not too disabled to play. There were the drifters on welfare in skuzzy jeans and windbreakers, and then there were the unemployed on social insurance. Quite the group. "Anyone seen Rick Miller? I want to talk to him."

"What about?" said a voice in the back. The voice belonged to a guy in his forties, medium height with a five o'clock shadow. Brown eyes stared at him belligerently.

"It's private. Can we have a word?"

"Yeah, where no one can hear us, eh? Come over to the corner where there's a table. We can sit there."

"I take it that you're Rick Miller?"

"So what?"

"Can you recall Friday. December thirteenth in the evening? Who did you shoot pool with?"

"A few guys."

"Was one of them Larry Smith?"

"Yeah, I played with him. Lost some money. I remember that game."

"When did it end?"

"Around 11p.m. and then I hung around and had a few beers."

"So you were here with him until midnight?"

"That's right. What's this about? What are you fishing for?"

"Just checking alibis. Who was with who. I'm investigating the Cathy Snifton murder case."

"Well, leave me out of it. I had nothing to do with it nor did Larry Smith."

"Yeah, so it appears. Thanks for your time." David got up to leave. Cross Larry Smith off my list.

Now to Knock Wood Furniture Store to see how Jones checked out. He easily found the store on Mississauga. A tall, thin man, wearing a red service jacket with the store's logo on the lapel approached him

"Can I help you? We've got some neat shovels on special or I can show you some bird feeders, great for attracting cardinals and blue jays. What are you interested in?"

"Are you Steve Jones or can you tell me where I can find him?"

"Yeah, I'm Steve Jones. What do you want?"

"I've come to ask you about where you were, December, the thirteenth, Friday, in the evening."

"Well, that's easy. I worked here until the store closed at nine p.m. and then my boss wanted me to do inventory. So I was here until after ten."

"Did you know Cathy Snifton?"

"Was that the girl that got murdered? Just what I read in the papers. Sad. I don't even know what she looked like."

"Her picture was in the paper."

"Well I've never seen her in here. What's it to you?"

"Just checking."

"Is it because of my previous record that you're here?"

"Yes, "

"Well I had nothing to do with it and my boss will verify

that I was here and then I went home."

David wrote his answer down in his book. Well if he hasn't lied, he was at the store working. Also if it's true that he doesn't know her, then there's no motive, he has no motive for killing her. There has to be a link between the victim and the killer

"Well then, I have no further questions," and he got up to leave.

"Sure you don't need a de-icer for your windshield? We have a special on that."

"No, I'm well taken care of in that respect." David headed out.

*****

He trudged back to the office through snow and on icy sidewalks that store owners had neglected to clear. He felt the snowflakes on his face and wiped them off with his gloves. By the time he got there his phone was ringing off the hook. He picked it up. "Is this David Scott in charge of the Cathy Snifton murder investigation?"

"I am at the moment. Who am I speaking to?"

"It's Mabel Day, wife of Reverend Day of Mariposa United. I know that you're a busy man and I hate to bother you, a man so busy as yourself."

"Do you know something about the murder?"

"Well no. You see my husband said that you had been in to see him the other day, asking him all kinds of questions. He got the impression, although he didn't come right out and say it, but he thought you considered him a suspect in that girl's murder. So I thought I would call and find out. Surely you don't suspect my husband, a man of the cloth?"

"Everyone in this town, Ma'am, is a suspect, regardless of race, religion, or creed until proven otherwise."

"Well I can vouch for him. He was home here with me the night Cathy Snifton was murdered."

"Between eleven p.m. and one a.m. was he there with you?" said David taking out his notebook.

"Of course he was with me. Where else could he have

83

possibly been?"

"You raised the question, Ma'am, not me. I have made a note of your statement. Thanks for your help." He hung up the phone.

Another meddling nosey parker, David thought.

Chapter 12

Whew! What a day! Winter always gets me down thought Clara Clarke. First her car wouldn't start. Then she arrived at school late. The kids were ratty. In her first class, sixteen-year-old Jason had reached down below his desk to rub his crotch several times. Puberty blues. She had chosen to ignore it, but the gesture irritated her just the same.

Now her key wouldn't turn in her front door lock because of the cold. Damn! The key finally turned and the door opened.

Clara threw her briefcase on the hall table then hung up her coat in the hall closet. She kicked off her boots. Next, she stooped down and picked up her mail from the rubber mat. It was mostly advertising flyers, hardly worth the effort. She threw them in the waste paper basket.

In the living room she sank down into the sofa and put her feet up on the coffee table. Now she could relax. But no sooner had she settled, than the doorbell rang.

Rats!

She got up to answer it.

It was Tom, his eyes twinkling good humouredly. He swept her up in a big hug with, "How's my favourite teacher today?" Like a magician he pulled out of his sleeve a big red apple.

"Oh, Tom," laughed Clara. "you tease! It's so good to see you. Come on in."

"Thanks, Clara. I thought I'd drop by and see how the world is treating my favourite teacher." He easily settled his lanky frame into the sofa. "That's a nice dress you have on. It becomes you. It compliments those lovely, big, brown eyes of yours."

"Oh, you flatterer," said Clara loving every bit of it. "Flattery will you get everywhere." She was obviously pleased with his compliments. Suddenly she didn't feel tired anymore. "How about a nice cup of coffee? It will just take a minute to put on and then I'll sit down."

"Sounds great, but let's get serious for a moment," said

Tom flopping down beside her on the sofa. "I can't believe what happened last Friday, Cathy's murder. I know she was your best friend and I want to say how sorry I am."

"Your friend too," corrected Clara.

"Yes and no," said Tom with studied casualness. "We dated but we weren't that close. I always trusted you more. More than I ever did her. I always felt closer to you, Clara. Hey, I've known you all my life. You're my neighbour," and he took her hand in his.

"You went out with Cathy for a long time," said Clara, moving a little away.

"Yes, I did, and I'm the first one to admit it was a mistake. I learned the hard way. But that's the past. The rumour I hear going around the town is that the police think it was someone she knew. The police think it was one of us. Have you heard anything?"

"Not a thing. Why would any one of us want to murder her? She was a sweet girl," replied Clara while quietly thinking that sweet was not quite the right adjective to describe Cathy. Adjectives such as adventurous and promiscuous would be more accurate. But she could afford to be kind, now that Cathy was dead.

Tom persisted. "They're trying to get alibis from all her friends."

"Why her friends? Why not her enemies?"

"Search me. But that's what the police are doing. I thought you might have heard something."

"No."

"Let's change the subject. Give me a hug for old time's sake and then I must be off."

At the door Tom paused, leaning his lanky frame against the door frame, "How about we neighbours get together this week, for old time's sake, like for dinner and a movie or something and get caught up on old times?"

"Oh, I'd love to Tom," said Clara, her eyes flashing. "I have been feeling a little down."

After Tom left, Clara hugged herself with joy. With Cathy out of the way Tom, the boy next door that she'd loved all her life, would be hers.

*****

Dave decided to catch Clara after school when she might speak more freely. He pulled up in front of her cottage. He was here, he reminded himself, to investigate Cathy's murder, nothing else. He stopped to admire the cottage's architecture. They sure don't make cottages the way they use to, he thought. Snow covered the long sloping roof. Below the eaves were two dormer windows. Over the front door was a large semi-circular window. Two vertical stained glass windows flanked either side of the solid oak door.

He lifted the heavy brass knocker and gave it a loud thump. A flash of golden hair appeared momentarily behind the window. Then the door opened.

In her stockinged feet, obviously puzzled and not expecting him, Clara blurted out, "Oh, it's you. I thought it might be..." her voice trailed off.

"It's cold standing here. May I come in?"

"My place is a mess. You're seeing me at my worst. I've just got in from school."

"No problem," said David, stepping inside, "you should see my apartment. It's always in a state."

He glanced briefly at the gold framed print of Redoute's botanical roses hanging on the wall before turning into the living room. Clara has good taste. In the living room corner, David spied a stereo with a compact disc player, something that he had put off buying. He wanted to go through her CD collection and see what her choice in music was, but he didn't have time. Clara indicated that he could sit down on the sofa. Just as he did so, he noticed two empty coffee cups sitting on the glass coffee table.

"This is a nice place that you have here."

"Thank you. You're the second person that has said that to me today."

Who was the other person, wondered David, probably a guy. Instead of asking, he said, "Clara can you find a seat and sit down. You're making me nervous, standing."

"Really? Making a policeman nervous? It is usually the

87

other way round," said Clara, sitting on a Queen Anne uphol-stered chair next to the fireplace. She turned to poke a cedar log further into the fire.

What a lovely profile, thought David, the long, straight nose, those lovely brown eyes and full lips. His eyes drifted downwards to her full breasts. Keep your mind on your work, you horny bastard.

"Clara, I have to ask you about your movements Friday night. You are not a suspect, but I am asking these questions to eliminate you."

"I was down at Brewery Bay early in the evening with the gang drinking and chatting. Then I drove home alone and went to bed. I don't know where the others went. I had a long, tiring day from teaching and wanted to get home."

"Clara, as one of Cathy's best friends, she must have confided in you a great deal, did she not?"

Clara turned to face him. "Yes, she told me things. But she didn't tell me everything. By nature, she was very secretive."

"But she must have told you some things, like whom she was in love with, whom she was going out with? Did she have any enemies or anyone who would want to do her harm?"

Clara shook her head. "She never spoke badly of anyone so I would assume she had no enemies, although we all irritate someone at any given time, but she didn't confide in me to that extent."

"Did she mention the names of the men in her life? Whom she was going out with?"

"Cathy hung out with James and Bob. I didn't know her private life."

"Did she go out with Ted Chirp?"

"I don't know."

"Tom.... What about Tom Ball?" David smiled at her.

There was an instant chill in the air. "Why don't you ask him?"

"Were Tom and Cathy lovers?"

"Friends," hissed Clara, "I'm sure they were JUST friends."

"Cathy was a hot blooded young woman. Her reputation in this town was not that of the vestal virgin."

"People act differently with different people." Clara was stumbling, a bright flush was creeping up her neck to her face.

Methinks the lady doth protest too much, thought David.

"What are you getting at? What are you trying to say?" demanded Clara.

"Cathy was three months pregnant when she was murdered. I think that's an important clue."

"Oh, no," said Clara, "Oh, no it can't be true. How awful."

"Her pregnancy is connected in some way, I believe, with her murder. Do you have any idea who the father might be? James Muir?"

Clara shook her head.

"Bob Thompson?"

"She stopped going with him a while ago."

"What about," David paused for effect, "Tom Ball, your next door neighbour?"

Clara jumped angrily to her feet. "Tom is my neighbour and friend. How can you sit here and accuse my friend that I've known since childhood, of murder? I won't listen to you anymore! Please leave."

Walking down the front sidewalk with the door angrily slammed behind him, David kicked at a piece of ice covered rock. So much for my interviewing techniques, I really blew that one. Like half the women in this town, she must be in love with that creep, Tom Ball. Me? Now I'm the nasty guy. Shit!

David slammed his car door shut and sat in the cold while the engine heated up. What a disastrous interview and now this numbing cold!

Back in his apartment he put his feet up and flicked on the cable TV station to get news flashes and weather predictions for tomorrow. Flurries expected late afternoon. Sun setting at five-thirty. What sun? There will be a high of minus 10 and a low of minus twenty. Wind chill factor minus thirty. The weather was a downer.

He thought over his conversation with Clara. She could have done it. It wouldn't have taken any great strength to strangle thin, wiry Cathy, especially if she were caught by surprise. Just tighten the scarf and put pressure on the neck. According to Dr. Frost, it doesn't take much to snap the hyoid bone. Her motive, that was easy. She wanted her childhood sweetheart back. With Cathy out of the way it would be clear sailing.

But how could Clara know that Cathy was in the park, unless Cathy had prearranged to meet her there. Cathy might have phoned her and asked for her help or advice earlier.

Cathy would be a real threat to Clara's future happiness if Cathy had confided in Clara that she was pregnant and that Tom was the father. Or if Clara had got wind of the fact that Cathy might try to blackmail Tom and get him to marry her.

The big question, was she sincere in how she reacted to my news that Cathy was pregnant, or did she know all along? Otherwise, she has no motive, and an alibi for earlier in the evening.

Chapter 13

Saturday morning, December, the twenty-first. A week has passed since the murder, thought David glumly, and I'm just beginning in my investigation. Every day brings a new suspect, a new motive. David figured his search was getting wider rather than narrower with each passing day. He quickly dressed and went down to the office to think about his suspects. Tom Ball, who had dated Cathy for years, had she tried to blackmail him about her pregnancy? Probably, because he had the money. Ted Chirp, known for his violent behaviour had also dated Cathy prior to her death. Both these men were prime suspects. Then there was George, a convicted wife killer, who had received a manslaughter charge, had finished his sentence and was working as a janitor down at the church where she sang in the choir. How was he connected to Cathy? And James, where did he fit into all this mess, a man scared of his own shadow, acting like a gay rabbit? Which one of these guys was the father of her child? The coroner would have a DNA tissue sample of the foetus. But he couldn't get a court order for all his suspects to deliver semen on demand. It could be half the town. So many questions and so few answers.

At noon, David stepped out of his office to get a breath of fresh air. The bells in the steeple of Mariposa United Church were peeling out, *Oh Little Town of Bethlehem, how still we see thee lie.*

How, David wondered, was he going to get through it all? Shoppers on Mississauga Street were side stepping around the deep snow drifts trying to do last minute Christmas shopping before Christmas Eve when the shops shut early. Last year, he had been one of them. He had gone into Stein's Jewellery Shop and bought his wife a small, gold, fourteen karat heart with a gold chain to celebrate the coming of their child. This year he had no-one to buy a present for. Stop feeling sorry for yourself. It won't get you anywhere.

He decided to go down to the park to question Tim, the rink guard, again to see if he remembered anything else. He parked his car in the parking lot, which was almost deserted. Over at the rink he could see that a bonfire had been built at the edge, so that skaters could warm their hands over the fire to keep warm, a nice gesture by the Parks and Recreation staff.

Some giggling school girls were throwing snowballs at one youth who was skating backwards across the ice sticking out his tongue at them. At the edge of the rink a toddler, who had fallen into a snow bank, was being helped to his feet by his mother. On a nearby park bench, a father was busy tying up his son's skates. No possibilities here. No one that David knew.

"Hi again." It was Tim the rink guard. David had been so intent on checking out the faces on the rink, he had failed to notice Tim approaching him from the rear.

"Tim, I need your help. Can you recall anything more about that evening of December 13th, the night that Cathy Snifton was murdered? Anything you didn't tell me?"

Tim nodded. "Yes, I did remember something after you had gone. I meant to give you a call, but I have been so busy. I don't know whether it's important or not, that's why I didn't rush over to your office. I did see Cathy being picked up by some guy several times. He used to read the newspapers while he waited in his car."

"What kind of a car did he drive?"

"A little blue Toyota."

"Tim, this is important. Was he in the parking lot the night of the murder?"

"I don't know. Friday night is a busy night and I can't tell you for sure."

"Have you seen that car in the parking lot since she was murdered, or seen him hanging around the park lately."

"No. I figured he was just there to pick Cathy up. I saw her get into his car once or twice."

"What did he look like?"

"I never got a good look at him. He was always reading the newspaper."

David wrote it all down. How many men in the town drove a blue Toyota? An interesting clue.

"Sometimes he came on his own. He'd just sit there in his car watching."

"How often did he come?"

"Several times a week, usually after work or around the supper hour. Sometimes in the evening. But he was always alone in his car looking at the skaters."

"Did you see him that Friday night, when Cathy was murdered?"

Tim shook his head. "Like I say, it was a busy night. No. The strange thing is that I haven't seen him hanging around here since. Maybe he will come back. Who knows?"

"What did he look like?"

"An older guy. I couldn't get a good look from the rink, it's some distance. He parked his car off to the side. An older guy."

"Did you see anyone else get out of his car or get into his car?"

"No, just Cathy. But after it gets dark around supper time it would be hard to see that far. It was only when he came around five that I noticed him."

"Thanks Tim, you've been a great help."

"I hope so. Everyone in town is pretty frightened with a murderer running around loose."

The blue Toyota was a great help. But how important is this loner sitting in his car? How strong a connection did he have with Cathy? Was she dating him? He might just be a poor, hard-working stiff, finding peace and quiet at the end of the day by relaxing in the park before going home to chaos and confusion. David headed back to his office. He decided to make it simple. Find out what cars his suspects drove. I bet one of them drives this car and if not, then he would have to start from scratch, a thought he didn't relish at all.

Chapter 14

On Monday morning, the twenty-third of December, Billy made a point of jogging past Miss Temple's cottage hoping to find her about. He wanted to discuss, diplomatically, the defacing of hymn books. He couldn't come right out and say, stop taking a ball point pen to them. He had to ask her in a circumspect way why she did this, proceeding very delicately. He could say that he'd seen her take her pen out of her purse during the service. He would tell her that he found it very flattering that she was going to make notes about his sermon. He would make sure that she got a reprint. She wouldn't need to take out her pen any more.

Dealing with Miss Temple required a great deal of tact

But on the sidewalk in front of her cottage, he found a very downcast Miss Temple on the verge of tears.

"What's wrong, dear?" inquired Billy putting his arm gently around her shoulders. He remembered the last time when he had tried to plant a kiss on her forehead and she had acted as if he had suggested sexual intercourse.

Miss Temple ducked to escape his embrace. "The word 'dear' is a very patronising term," huffed Miss Temple, slightly out of breath. "I have a speck in my eye that I am trying to get out." An uncontrolled tear splashed down Miss Temple's cheek.

"Here, tilt your chin up and let me take a look at that eye," said Billy, as he gently tilted her head back. "Look up at the sky. Now look to your left. Good! Now look to your right." He could find nothing, not an eyelash not even a speck of dirt in her eye.

"I can't see anything," he said after a pause, "and I am looking very hard. Roll your eyeball heavenward."

Miss Temple stifled a sob, trying to maintain her dignity as two large tears rolled slowly down her parched, wrinkled, cheeks. "My cat, Diefenbaker, was found this morning. He had been.... Oh it's too horrible to mention... some nasty person has strangled my cat!"

"Oh, how perfectly dreadful," said Billy, hoping that he

had put the right amount of shock and sorrow into his voice. He felt like such a hypocrite. Inwardly he thanked God for sending that very filthy obese cat without bladder control to its happy hunting ground. "

"Amen," he said quietly with head bowed.

"Do you think? Would it be possible?" Miss Temple was jerking at the sleeve of his jacket, "for you.... Do you think you could say a little prayer for my cat? I hope that there is something akin to our heaven for a cat."

He wanted to say, "Over my dead body," but Billy quickly said, "Of course, Miss Temple. Your cat was one of God's creatures. Just like the hymn, *God sees the little sparrow fall*. God sees everything and cares for every living creature, even, uh, your cat, Diefenbaker. It was a dastardly deed," said Billy, "only a craven coward would do such a thing."

Miss Temple look more relieved and nodded her head, "Thank you."

Since her expression had cheered up somewhat Billy decided to proceed on his delicate mission, "Miss Temple, dear Miss Temple, can I ask you something? How do you feel about the hymns we sing? Do you find them... inspirational?"

"Of course I do, Reverend Day!" exclaimed Miss Temple looking up at him with a puzzled expression.

"Mm," said Reverend Day, "in what way?"

"They lift the spirit and the heart. But," she cocked her head to one side, "since you asked me, I wasn't going to bring this up, but I will. What I don't like are some of the words. 'O Brother man, fold to thy heart, thy brother.' As a man, you might not find the language oppressive. You might not find anything offensive in the hymn, '*Onward Christian Soldiers marching off to war.*' But I do. I don't like the war images in our hymns. I don't like the use of militaristic language. For example, that hymn, '*Rise up, Oh Future Kings. Take up Thy Swords, to rake and beat up.*' These are violent images. Language is made violent by its repeated use. The church is using militaristic images and male symbols in our service of worship.

"We are using violent male images and the more we use them, the more violent our behaviour becomes with their use, the more violent our society becomes.

"There is constant reference to God as being a father figure and male. We use such phrases as 'we live in His world'. God may be a female. Have you, yourself, seriously considered this? You, Reverend Billy," and she pointed her arthritic bent finger at his nose, "you fail to see language and its use as a justice issue."

"I fail to see..." said Reverend Day in what he hoped was his mildest voice. What was the connection? What was the old dear going on about anyway? First it was the death of her cat, and now it was a justice issue. Really, the things that old ladies think up these days. Why didn't they sit in a corner and knit? Why couldn't Miss Temple be a sweet, harmless old lady, of trouble to no one?

"The point is, and there is a point," said Miss Temple, "we have had a violent death in our community. Cathy Snifton, a church choir member was murdered. She met a violent end. The use of violence in our language may have created a climate leading up to this. Look at what happened to my cat."

"Really, Miss Temple," said Reverend Day, exasperated, "what you are saying is that Cathy's death is connected with expressions that have been used for over two hundred years in our hymn books. Don't you find this all far-fetched? Why, I can remember my poor, dear mother.... God rest her soul," sighed Billy, "singing them to me as a child while she put me to bed at night. She had the loveliest Scottish voice. She sang like an angel."

"Songbook, PLEASE!," corrected Miss Temple. "I don't want it called a hymn book. If we start today to cut out our violent language, images and expression, then we will have a peaceful society based on all-inclusive language. I'm doing my part. Are you doing YOURS?" said Miss Temple, peering up at him.

"I see," said Billy, but he didn't really. "I have to keep running, Miss Temple, or I'll freeze to death," and he leaped out along the path ahead of her.

"Think about the language," Miss Temple called after him.

Hymns that he learned at his mother's knee were militaristic? Oh, come on now. Where was she getting her ideas? Was

96

she getting them at the United Church Women's meetings and their consciousness raising sessions? He would check again with Mabel as to their latest interests and topics of conversation. Was there a growing feminist movement amongst the United Church Women? He shook his head. Better not to stir the pot. The best thing was to let the matter ride, unless it became an issue. So Miss Temple wants to scribble in a few hymn books. Let her. An eccentric habit. He, Reverend Day, had more pressing concerns.

As he continued to jog along, a ray of hope entered his heart. During Christmas Day, when Mabel liked to lie down for an afternoon nap, he'd go for a run and drop into Gale's place for a little solace. He'd remembered her remark when he'd bumped into her in the shopping mall. She'd bubbled with obvious delight about her purchase. "I've bought a plump butterball turkey. I'm going to let it thaw out the night before and then get up very early Christmas morning, and pop it into the oven. Are you doing the same?"

"Nothing exciting. Mabel is serving, just fish." Maybe it was the way he said it, with a downcast air, and Gale had quickly picked up the hint and said, "Drop by. I'll save some dressing and a turkey breast for you."

He remembered the cute teddy bear decal on her refrigerator door, 'Have you given your child a hug today?' Billy had no child to hug. He wanted to hug Gale, that's who he wanted to hug. Billy decided that Christmas was not going to be so bleak after all.

Chapter 15

David decided to drop into the Mississauga Street Flower shop and have a chat with James. He didn't think he'd get much information, but at least James would verify Tom Ball's alibi for the night of the thirteenth.

Mississauga Flower Shop was easy to find. David opened the door, setting off a series of bird chimes. Freshly cut bouquets of freesia, pink carnations, red and white roses, which were very expensive at any time of year. Carnations of all colours stood in aluminium pails of water by the door.

The scent of pine wreaths, pine cones, and pot pourri sitting around in scattered peanut sized bowls was overwhelming. It was hard to keep from sneezing.

Big, red velvet bows sat in the middle of potted red and pink poinsettias and white mums. Overkill, thought David.

Lifelike artificial birds, with little white tags on their ankles, 'Made in China', sat in twig-lined nests. They were too cute for words.

James was nowhere to be found.

At the back of the store, David found a thin youth with a spiked orange hairdo and a small gold earring in his left ear carefully making a floral arrangement by sticking the stems of red carnations into a large crystal glass holder.

"I'm looking for James Muir, any idea where I can find him?"

The youth twisted his mouth in a look of contempt. "Not seen him for a little while. Probably gone home to help feed his bleeding mother. She's always on the phone to us."

"Do you know his home address?"

"He lives at 22 Simcoe Street, not far from the park."

"Thanks."

"You're welcome."

David drove along Simcoe, not far from the downtown area, to a series of houses near the railroad tracks. He found 22 Simcoe to be a modest two-storey, white frame house, sitting in a row of identical frame houses, one right after the other, with no distinguishing features. It was so plain, it was depressing. A small front porch contained overturned chairs covered in plastic to protect them from the winter elements. He walked up the front path and rang the front door bell. He waited while the sound of a man's footsteps came down the hall to the door.

It was James, wearing an apron over his jeans, and elbow-length yellow washing up gloves. James noticed his glance at the gloves.

"You've caught me at a bad time. What do you want?" He wiped his hands on his apron. "I'm in the middle of washing up the breakfast dishes."

"May I come in? I need to ask you more details about December, the thirteenth."

James' face turned pale. He nodded towards the kitchen. "We can talk back there without my mother upstairs hearing us. It's lucky you caught me in. I'm usually at work during the day, but I take a long lunch hour so that I can make mother's lunch and get things cleaned up around here."

David followed James down the worn and faded linoleum covered hall to the kitchen at the back of the house. A brief glance at the refrigerator and the stove with no timing mechanisms, told David that they were at least thirty years old, if not more. He could smell the vegetable soup simmering on the front burner. Several slices of whole wheat bread lay on the breadboard. A plastic bowl and a plate, a paper napkin and large spoon were placed on the tray in readiness. James pulled out a plain wooden chair for David to sit on. He slipped the apron over his head, took off his rubber gloves and hung them up to dry on a hook near the sink. Outside the kitchen window, David noticed some chickadees had come to the birdfeed station for some suet.

"James, going back to that evening in the park the night of Cathy's murder, will you describe again your movements? I want every detail again from the beginning."

James' Adam's apple bobbed in his throat, as he put his hand up to cover a cough. "I wish to God that I had been with Cathy and that I had protected her. This never would have happened. I blame myself."

"You weren't alone in the park were you? You were with

99

someone else."

James got up abruptly and went over and emptied out the dirty washing up water from the basin.

"You were with Neary, the church organist, weren't you? Don't lie, James, a lie will get you nowhere."

"Who told you? Tom Ball, wasn't it? He's the one who saw me in the park. Okay, I was with Neary. We couldn't go back to his house because his mother was over here from Scotland for the holidays. We couldn't go back to my house because of my mother. Where else could we go? We hit upon the idea of going to the park."

From the upstairs, David heard the shaking of a bell and the querulous voice of an old lady yelling, "What's keeping you, James. Where's my lunch?"

James looked at David meekly. "Do you mind if I take her lunch up to her? It will take just a few minutes."

David nodded.

James returned and slumped into his chair. David saw his pulse beating in his neck and drops of sweat on his brow. "The news will be all over town. Tom will tell everybody that Neary and Muir had it off in the park. When the news reaches my mother, it will kill her. I've never told her that I'm gay. My mother she thinks I am normal like everyone else. Can't you see the predicament that I'm in?"

James began blabbing the story of his life. One secret led to another, bubbling up suddenly like a spring in the ground, never stopping. David didn't particularly want to hear it but there was no stopping James.

"You don't know how hard I wanted to be normal and like everyone else. You don't know how often I prayed to God before I went to bed at night that I would wake up in the morning cured.

"I've always felt different, even as a child. When I was four or five I was sexually molested by my next door neighbour. Mother wasn't aware of what was going on. As a child, you can't tell. I was too afraid to tell, too ashamed. Would she have believed me if I had told her? She might have said, it's just your imagination.

"My father," said James bitterly, "ran off when I was a

baby. We don't know where he is. I guess that I've always been looking for my father in other men. I've always been searching for love.

"In High School, I thought things would be different. But all my sexual fantasies were about other guys. Several older men made passes at me, but I rejected them. I was not like them, I told myself. When I went out with the gang, I desperately wanted to be just like one of them. I joined in when they talked and jeered about queers and faggots.

"I tried to be normal. I did everything to be normal. My mother wanted me to go out with a nice girl. Cathy was just a front, the one girl that my mother approved of in this town. But I really did care for Cathy. She was a good friend. She was the only one that understood me." James stifled a sob.

"How did you meet Neary?"

"I met Neary in the Opera House, after a concert, in the men's washroom. He kept staring at me. I followed him out of the washroom. I needed love from another man," said James, turning his burning face away from David, "and I thought that I'd found it. My first and only lover. If I hadn't been busy with Neary in the park, I might have been able to save Cathy that night," James' voice trailed off.

"Get hold of yourself, calm down. No one could have foreseen that she would have been murdered in the park. What time did you leave the park? Did you see anyone besides Tom Ball?"

"We left around 10:30. I was too embarrassed to notice anyone. I just wanted to get away, out of there. That's all I can tell you." James' eyes were bloodshot.

David put away his notebook. "We can't keep knocking ourselves for events that happened in the past. Why don't you have a pastoral chat with Reverend Day."

"Him? He's only interested in chatting up the ladies. He wouldn't take any interest in the likes of me."

"I see," said David. But he didn't quite see. It was James' problem. Be a man, not a wimp. He felt sorry for James and he wished that he could do something. But what could he do? Nothing. But at least it confirmed and provided an alibi for Neary and James. But what if Tom hadn't come right home

101

when he said he had. What if he'd stayed in the park to meet Cathy? There was that possibility.

"Did you see Tom Ball leave the park? Did you see in what direction he headed?"

"No. We just wanted to get the hell out of there. Neary drove to my place and he let me out." James looked at his watch, "Oh, migawd. I'll be late at work. Can I go now?"

"Sure, James, no problem." David closed his notebook and headed for the front door.

James' account confirmed Neary's alibi and that of Tom Ball being in the park. But it still left the question of Tom Ball's alibi open ended. Did anyone see him leave the park? Did he do what he said he did, go straight home?

Chapter 16

David looked at his watch. Five o'clock. Friday. It was Happy Hour down at Brewery Bay. He decided it was as good a time as any to mingle with the regulars, pick up the local gossip and talk to Tony, the bar tender, to confirm who had been in last Friday night. Maybe he would recall something.

Brewery Bay was right on Mississauga down from Apple Annie's. It had a long bar in front and a restaurant in back.

Several couples were sitting at small tables near a wood-burning fire. He remembered that in another bar, a Scottish one, a wood burned tableau on the wall had caught his eye, the tale of the Scottish King, Robert the Bruce. Discouraged and down hearted, the King was sitting in his room watching a small spider in a corner try to weave a web. Three times the spider was unsuccessful. But the fourth time it made it. Just thinking about the tale made him keep going.

"I just hope the number of Cathy's friends doesn't mean interviewing half the town," he thought.

"Excuse me," he said to a burly farmer blocking his way. "Shure thing," the man slurred. "Hey fellas," the farmer shouted so anyone within hearing distance would hear, "make way for this thirsty man."

David gave him a black look, which had absolutely no effect on the man at all, and took a seat at the end of the bar.

"Tony, Fridays really get me down."

"Yeah, same here. But don't let the day of the week get to you. A young woman in Chicago went out and killed three people because she found Mondays depressing. What will you have?"

"An Upper Canada light. What did Cathy Snifton usually order?"

"A spritzer."

"I'm investigating her murder. Any ideas?"

Tony shrugged. "It could be anyone. Somebody probably forgot to return a library book. Instead of paying the fine, they decided to bump her off. Just kidding." He laughed at his little joke.

"I heard that she came in Fridays regularly, with the crowd. Where did they sit?"

"Over there at that table."

"Who was she usually with?"

"Tom Ball, James Muir, Bob Thompson, Clara and sometimes Ted Chirp."

Ted Chirp, the guy who was up on a wife battering charge, whose wife didn't press charges.

"What about the night she was murdered? Who showed up that night?"

"Mm, let me see now," Tony stopped polishing the glass and put it down. "I don't believe I saw her. I'm so used to seeing her come in that I take for granted that she came. That's right! She never showed up. Her friends waited for a while and then came over to the bar and asked if there were any telephone messages from Cathy. Tom Ball came in late. Clara, the school teacher, was already there. James was over on the side talking to Mr. Neary, the organist." He gave David a wink. "It wasn't like Cathy to miss having a drink with the gang."

"Who else of that crowd didn't show up that evening?"

"Bob Thompson, the other school teacher, didn't show up. Ted Chirp came in later."

"Then what happened?"

"Around 8 p.m. they all got up and left. Tom said something about feeding his dog. James accepted a lift from Neary. Clara had her own car. It's too bad about Cathy. She was nice and friendly to me. If you want to speak to Ted Chirp, he's over there nursing a beer. Dreadful," said Tony shaking his head. He returned to polishing the glasses.

"If you remember anything, give me a call." David handed him his card.

The tall, lanky figure of Ted Chirp was sprawled out in a chair watching CNN News. His black leather jacket was draped over the back of the chair. His black hair was long, reaching his collar. Below his right eyebrow was a small scar. He looked to be in his early forties.

"Mind if I join you?" It was more a command than a request.

"No problem. I don't own the place. If I did there might be a problem." Ted lifted his boots off the chair in front of him and kicked the chair towards him.

David flashed his badge.

"Official stuff, huh?"

"I came to talk to you about Cathy Snifton."

"Why do you want to ask me?" asked Ted belligerently.

"I want a few answers. Did you go out with her?"

"Yeah, and so did half the town."

"Don't be a smart-ass with me, or I'll take you in and book you for obstructing justice."

"Look, I'll co-operate. But what I tell you will I hope be confidential." Ted briefly glanced around to make sure that no one was listening.

"This is a murder investigation, not a National Enquirer interview."

Ted chewed his lip. "The reason I need confidentiality is that I'm trying to get back with the little woman. You know how things are." He winked at David. "News of my involvement with Cathy wouldn't help matters. Besides, Cathy is dead. The past is the past. I have to get on with my life."

What a selfish creep thought David. Get on with his life. A young woman has been killed and that's all he thinks about.

"Did you go out with her?"

"Yeah, I used to go out with her. Nothing serious. I'm a married man. My wife wouldn't like it. I'm having enough problems with her as it is. Going out with Cathy, it was just for kicks. I liked Cathy. But come on," he smiled conspiratorially at David, "you know what it's like."

"No, I don't know what it's like," replied David. "How did you meet?"

"Cathy lingered behind one Friday night. I picked her up. If you knew Cathy, that wasn't difficult. She had no objections to going out with me, a married man."

"How did you keep in touch with her? Did you phone her at home or work?"

"Silly question, at work of course. Never at home with that old harridan mother of hers. I phoned her at the library. We'd meet after work, or after she finished skating over at the park."

"I'm curious," said David, "what was the attraction?"

"At first I was attracted to Cathy because of her sweetness. I had all kinds of problems at home. She was a good listener. I felt that I could tell her anything. Cathy was very sympathetic and very understanding."

"Did you give her any details about the beatings you gave your wife or did you leave that out?"

Chirp gave him a hard stare. David waited and then asked, "Where did you like to go on your dates with Cathy?"

"Around. Drives in the country. Small places, nothing fancy. Sometimes just take-out places, if I was short of cash."

"What was Cathy really like?"

Ted sneered. "You don't know?"

"No, Tell me."

"She was a hot one. A good fuck. On the outside she looked like the Virgin Mary, all sweetness and innocence. But that was all a cover up. She'd drop her panties at the drop of a dime. Sometimes I figured that it was all that repression bottled up in her, living in that fleabag of a house with that old hag, her mother. She could never have her friends over. She never lived a normal life."

"You never went to her house?"

"Never. That's the way she wanted it. I never met her mother and I don't know if she had any other family to speak of. I guess what Cathy wanted was lots of attention and affection. Instead she got sex. She confused the issues. From me she got sex. I didn't abuse her. She offered it and I took it. Other than sex, we had nothing in common."

"Sure you had something in common. Figure it out," snapped David. "When was the last time you saw her?"

"About three weeks ago."

"Aw, come on. You had a good thing going and the last time you saw her was three weeks ago?"

"I had problems to sort out at home," said Ted looking at his feet and shifting in his chair.

He's lying, thought David.

"Don't leave town. I want you available for further questioning. I am not satisfied with your answers."

106

"You know where to find me."
"Yeah, under a rock."

Chapter 17

Saturday morning, he felt a slight buzz from the night before. He'd had too many beers while interviewing Ted Chirp. Deep in thought, he heard Mira's voice long before he saw her face in the outer office asking for him. He felt a little guilty. He hadn't been deliberately avoiding her since the funeral. He had just been too busy. Her boots clomped confidently along the corridor towards him.

"Hi," said Mira, her cheeks glowing from the cold. "Almost a week since the funeral. Almost a week since I saw you last. Five days make a woman weak," she sighed. "I thought I'd drop by and see how this busy boy, that means you, is doing. I wanted to make sure that you were among the living."

"If you're trying to make me feel guilty, Mira, then you've succeeded," replied David, getting to his feet. "I don't have to explain to you that I have to work around the clock until this murder is solved."

"No, tell me again," said Mira playfully reaching out to grab at his tie and pull on it.

David caught her hand. "Come on. Let's slip over to Apple Annie's for a coffee."

"That's big of you."

"Don't be cruel," said David.

To have more privacy and to avoid the crowd at the front of the shop, David led her to a booth at the back.

"Fill me in on the latest," commanded Mira. "There should be no secrets between friends."

"I'm interviewing Cathy's closest friends. Her male friends, Tom, Dick and Harry as the expression goes. Which one did it? I haven't a clue. The investigation is continuing. Will that satisfy you?"

"Mm. A little. Like a bird, a few crumbs are all I get from you, David," she reached under the table and pressed her hand on his knee. "I know that you're a competent and thorough investigator. It's not your work that I am worried about. You're a workaholic. You're not taking time out for a little R and R.

Come back to my place tonight. It will inspire you and give you more ideas," whispered Mira, "I'll keep a light burning in the window, like those old lighthouses of yore, and the coffee pot on the boil."

"Mira, please," said David. "I've got to work on this case. I am nowhere near to solving it. Have mercy."

"Have you heard the old saying?" replied Mira, "Time and tide wait for no man. Think about it. I'll wait up for you. Come, I'll be waiting."

"Mira, you're asking the impossible."

*****

Gale Chirp had just put her aching feet up on a footstool in front of the TV. It had been a long day. It was time to catch up on the news. But just as she picked up the remote control, she heard a light tapping on the window. She looked toward the space where the living room drapes didn't close. She saw the fist of a white hand taping on the glass. She jumped up. Her heart beat faster. Cathy Snifton's murderer had not been caught. She was a woman, alone in a house with two children. Reaching for the phone and holding the extension cord in her left hand, she stood beside the wall and, with a newspaper, moved the living room curtain a little to see who it was.

Gale had been hoping that Billy would drop by for a late cup of coffee, but Billy wouldn't tap on the window like that. Billy would ring the doorbell.

Gale couldn't see anyone. So she next went out into the hall and turned on the porch light to get a better look. It was Ted standing there looking straight at her.

What does that son of a bitch want? Why has he called at this late hour, scaring me half to death? Keep your cool. Stay calm.

Keeping the latch on, she opened the door a few inches. "Hello, what brings you here?" If he was drunk, she would slam the door in his face.

"Hello? Is that any way to greet your husband? Just a hello?"

Ted wedged his foot in the door space. "Don't be hostile,

Gale, I've come to apologize. I want to tell you how truly I hate myself for what I did to you in front of the kids. You don't know how sorry I am. It hurt me more than I can ever say. I'm truly, truly sorry for hitting you, Gale. I can never ever express how badly I feel about what happened."

Gale pursed her lips. She didn't know what to say or to do. Ted continued to plead. "I need to talk to you, Gale. You don't know how depressed I've been feeling. Living without you and the kids is awful. Life hasn't been worth living. Please, please, Gale, can't I come in for a few minutes? I'll just come in for a few minutes and then go."

It was a difficult decision, but Gale decided that a few minutes wouldn't hurt if he'd promise then to go and leave her alone. She took the latch slowly off the door and let him in, saying, as a further reason for him not to stay long, "I haven't finished with my housework and ironing things for the kids. I'm really surprised that you would have the nerve to show your face around here after what happened. You almost killed me."

Ted slipped into the hall and followed Gale into the living room. "Gale, honey, I said I was sorry. How many times do I have to say it? It will never happen again. I promise." He tried to lift her chin to his face, but she broke free and headed into the kitchen. "I'll put on some coffee."

"A friend of mine suggested that I go to Alcoholics Anonymous meetings to find out why I need to drink. I went to my first meeting last night."

"That's a step in the right direction."

Gale pulled the ironing board out of the cupboard. Next she picked up the steam iron and went over to the sink to fill it. By ironing she could keep her emotions in control. She rummaged around in the laundry basket and seized her daughter's white blouse, straightening it out with her hands. Then she lightly touched the iron to see if it was ready.

"I couldn't stay away, Gale. I had to come by and see how you were doing. I miss you and the kids."

Gale shrugged her shoulders. and continued ironing. She watched him wander around the kitchen, stopping to look at the splashed finger paintings done by the children tacked to the kitchen wall, the framed kindergarten picture of their daughter,

Tessa, with her classmates. After a cursory glance at her monthly calendar and reminders of things to do, held in place by a magnet bug to the refrigerator door, Ted walked into the living room and picked up their wedding picture in its sterling silver frame and brought it out to the kitchen.

"It seems so long ago," sighed Ted.

"A lot of water has gone over the dam," said Gale quietly before taking it from him and putting it back again on the living room mantle. He sat down again at the kitchen table and drummed his fingers on the wooden surface. "I find it so hard to relax. I can't even sit in a chair for long periods of time. My nerves aren't good. Gale."

"Coffee won't help."

Ted gave a wry grimace. "I've been so lonely without you. Don't you miss me? How can you live alone in this big house?" Ted went over to the kitchen window and looked out into the snowy night. "They haven't caught the murderer yet. He's still running around loose. A woman should not be home alone on her own."

"I keep the doors and windows locked. I'm very careful. I don't go out at night."

"I'm glad to hear that. I'm staying with a friend, an old widow. She's glad to have a man on the premises. She says it makes her feel more secure. But I don't want to stay there long. It's only a temporary arrangement. How about you? Are you managing? Have you been okay?"

"So, so. It was very hard at first. I've found it very hard to cope."

"Gale," he reached his hand across the table and touched her arm. "Can you find it in your heart to forgive me?"

Gale shivered and backed away. "It's too soon." said Gale, looking down at her hands. She had to be gentle so as not to provoke another outburst of rage. She couldn't risk another fight.

"Give me time to think things over, Ted. I have to think about things and have time to myself. You, too have to give yourself time. I think it's wonderful that you're going to A.A. Have you thought of therapy when you feel depressed and stressed out?"

"Yeah, someone suggested that. But I wouldn't be depressed, Gale, if I were back here with you." Gale brushed off his suggestion with, "Take each day, one step at a time."

"I know, I know," said Ted sharply.

Gale picked up his coffee cup. "I've got a big day ahead of me tomorrow. I've got to get some sleep. I've got to say good night now." Gale walked to the front door and opened it.

Ted threw up his arms. "Gale, you've got everything, the house, the kids. What have I got? Nothing," Ted kicking a children's snow boot out of his way in the hall. He pulled the collar of his leather jacket up and took a scarf out of his jacket pocket.

"I've got to go out into the cold winter night. Thanks, but no thanks," said Ted bitterly. "Think about it, Gale, There's a murderer on the loose and you're living here alone with the kids. You might be next."

Breathing a sigh of relief, Gale congratulated herself on getting Ted out of the house before he turned nasty. After she had shut and bolted the door and checked to see that all the downstairs windows were locked and the porch light was turned off, Gale realized that she was shaking all over. What a fool she'd been to take such a chance in letting him into the house this evening. What if he had refused to go home? What if he had turned nasty? He was so volatile. Anything could set him off. The next time she might not be so lucky. He could easily kill her in a rage. What would the children do without her? There must be no further invitations into the house.

Chapter 18

Christmas Eve. The church women were bustling inside the church getting it ready for the Christmas Eve Service. Tall, red candles in brass candlesticks had been placed in the nave, fir branches with big red velvet bows were hung at the bottom of the stained glass windows. The lights for the tall Christmas tree had been turned on. Red poinsettias had been set up on the steps leading up to the altar. A large wreath with four candles, symbolising the Four Sundays in advent, was placed next to the pulpit.

Early in the morning, George had turned the heat up to warm up the church, which usually took a couple of hours. Then he'd taken the vacuum cleaner upstairs and vacuumed all the rugs, all those loose pine needles that had dropped from the boughs and branches and the mud and snow that had been tracked in. After that he went outside. He'd been using the snow blower in the parking lot and on the sidewalks all day, clearing away the freshly fallen snow that piled up almost as fast as he removed it. The sidewalk would be covered again. It was frustrating. On the church steps, at the front and side doors, and the entrance off the parking lot, he'd made a special effort to make sure they were all nicely cleared off, and plenty of salt and sand spread so that. the elderly wouldn't trip and fall. Ice accumulated so quickly. Keeping busy kept his mind occupied. George was worried.

He was on a life-long probation to keep away from alcohol. He was getting on okay with his job, helping out as much as possible. He'd heard of no complaints. But now this girl had been murdered, a member of the church choir, and, the way the cops came around so quickly afterwards to interview him, they must suspect him. Cops are all the same. They come to you, acting so innocent, politely asking you the same questions over and over again hoping that you'll slip up and change your story. I've done time and I've paid my dues. But you're never off the hook with them. You're the first one they call on. Your rap sheet is always in the computer for violent crime. I'm the first one that they come looking for. Sometimes they never tell you what they are looking for. They just keep snooping and asking questions. They're trying to frame me. At my last job I was doing good. Then there was this assault on a woman at work, a rape on her way home. Next thing I knew the cops were on my doorstep. First they interviewed me at my place of work and then, on the way out, they had a little chat with my boss. They told him all the nice things about me. A couple of hours later my boss calls me in, for a chat. I knew what he was going to say. It was all over his face. The cops had told him about my conviction. He didn't say I did this new rape, but he said, "You have to understand my predicament, the safety of the female staff that work here. It's a sensitive situation." He didn't want a con working for him. I guess that I'll lose this job, too, thought George bitterly.

He decided to straighten out the hymn books and put the church calendars in neat piles at the entrance doors. Then he got a ladder and put up the order of hymns on the platform at the front. So many things had to be done and it took his mind off his personal problems and the worry that he would lose this job. He stood back to admire his efforts.

Now the church looked beautiful. The lovely bright reds of the flowers and the velvet ribbons, the smell of pine and spruce and the twinkling lights of the Christmas tree, it had been worth it.

He placed the large carton for food donations in a prominent position in the vestibule, with the cardboard sign above it, *'I was hungry and you fed me'*. George made sure it wasn't too close to the door. He remembered the wino who had ducked in the door, clamped his hand on a bag of groceries and was gone before anyone could stop him. Later, George had seen him on Main Street trying to flog the same groceries for money to buy booze.

George stepped outside to get a breath of fresh air. The wind had died down. Everything was crisp and still. A full moon was overhead. Just like the night when that girl was murdered. He shuddered at the thought of it.

114

Chapter 19

Soft, powdered snow was falling again. Deep snow drifts hugged both sides of the roads making visibility difficult at street corners. The snow plows had been out earlier in the day but the roads were becoming unmanageable again. On Mississauga the shops had begun closing early, one after another—Ball Haberdashery, Real Deal Real Estate, Apple Annie's, Mariposa Market—they had turned out the lights, locked their doors and put a *Closed for the Holiday* sign up at the windows. There was so much to do; get home, wrap the presents, get the meal on, and get ready for the big day. David stepped out of his office to see an almost deserted street, all the parked cars had gone. Only the lights at the intersection flashed on and off.

Greg and Clancy had invited him out for a quick drink after work, but he had declined, it would just make him feel worse. It would make him feel lonelier after they had left for their families.

High on the hill, the bells of St. Andrews Presbyterian pealed out, *O little town of Bethlehem, how still we see thee lie*. For David, as he tramped up the sidewalk to his apartment building, it was one of the loneliest nights of the year. He had bought some liquor and now he wanted to get blind drunk so that he would awaken in the morning having forgotten everything. He opened the door, turned up the heat, and looked around the apartment. There was not one decoration, nothing to show that it was Christmas. What would have been the point? Who would he have been decorating it for? No one came to visit.

He put in a long distance call to his parents who lived in Montreal, and wished them the best. His mother began crying, "You should spend Xmas with us and not be alone by yourself." But he had a murder investigation and he had to hang in until it was solved. His parents felt sorry for him. That made things much worse.

Around midnight, after a few stiff slugs of scotch, he fell

asleep on the sofa, listening to the FM station playing Christmas music softly in the background.

He was awakened by loud banging on his door. Rousing himself and wondering what time it was, he looked at his watch. It was 9:30 a.m. It was now Christmas Day. Who could it be?

Tousle haired and groggy he went to the door. He was in no shape for company. "I'm coming. Don't get your shorts in a knot."

It was fat Clancy, covered in snow, with a big red wrapped paper box under his arm. "HO! HO! HO! I'm Santa's elf. The Salvation Amy has a box for all good girls and boys. I thought I would bring you one. You've been a very good boy, David.

"I had some free time this morning to come over. We've finished opening our presents. My wife is getting the turkey ready and the kids are watching TV. My daughter was given two hamsters and a jungle gym set for Christmas. I went to the pet store last night and bought them. They assured me that they were two male hamsters. I thought two would keep each other company. Well Buddy has turned out to be a Pamela and has given birth this morning to ten babies. I am not feeding twelve hamsters. You'd think that after all these years of selling animals they could tell the sex of a hamster."

"Oh, you do have problems, Clancy, twelve hamsters in one cage. That'll be a bit crowded."

"Oh no, back to the pet store go the ten baby hamsters. I want my money back for fraud and misrepresentation. Oh, by the way, my daughter just loves it. She wants to keep all of them. So I told my wife, I need a break, go for a little drive and here I am. Now for the box," and he handed it over to David.

"You shouldn't have, Clancy. I haven't anything for you."

"Christmas is all about giving."

He opened the box. Inside was a pair of socks, some nice smelling soap and a bottle of Scotch.

"Very generous of you, Clancy," said David taking out the bottle to look at it more closely. I don't think the Salvation Army puts bottles in their Christmas boxes."

116

"Some do, some don't. This is a special occasion. You're welcome to come over for turkey dinner around 5 p.m. We have a place set for you at the table."

"That's kind of you, but I think I'll just wait it out. Thanks for coming and thanks for the gift."

Then Clancy was gone

After Clancy had left David felt hungry, so he made himself an unexciting tuna sandwich. He came out of the kitchen and looked over at the sofa. It would be tempting to snuggle up there and forget about being alone, without a wife and a child.

A snowball smacked his living room window. He looked out. It was Mira standing below on the snow covered front lawn. He opened the window.

"Let me in. I'm freezing out here. I cooked a turkey and brought it over thinking you and I can share it. I don't want to eat it alone. I'm feeling lonely and neglected, David, over at my place with my dying plants. That's not a good feeling to have Christmas Day. So I thought you and I should get together. Misery loves company."

He felt a little sorry for tough egg Mira. She'd seemed to have the skin of a rhinoceros and this was Christmas, the season of good will and cheer.

"Come on up."

Mira bounced in carrying a large shopping bag filled with plastic bowls. "Hold the door, take these while I get the turkey from the trunk of my car."

"That's good of you, Mira It's not what I expected. Clancy invited me over to his house but the noise and the kids would be too much for me."

"Set the table," ordered Mira, "quick, while the turkey is still hot. I just took it out of the oven. I'll get you to carve."

After carving the turkey, David went over to the sideboard and got out the good china dinner plates, the silver condiment holders and two crystal wine glasses, all wedding gifts, and put them on the table. He reached into the back of a drawer and hauled out two red candles. He put them into two candlestick holders. He lit the wicks and placed them on the table. They gave a soft, warm glow to the room. Looking at the table, he thought, it's beginning to feel like Christmas. Somewhere in the wine rack, he found a bottle of nice red wine that he had been saving for special occasions and brought it out. "What about cranberry jelly?"

"I brought some, along with gravy, potatoes, peas and turnips. We will have a feast." Mira looked at the table approvingly.

She placed the turkey, complete with stuffing, on a large serving plate before him. It looked delicious.

"Would you like the parson's nose?"

"Not really."

"Well then a leg or a breast?"

"Either. It all looks so good. That was a nice thing for you to do Mira, to bring this over."

"Well, while everything is hot, let's dive in. I should tell you, David, I just brought over the first course. We'll have to use our imagination for the second. I also thought, let's skip dessert. Coffee will be good enough. We don't need dessert, do we?" She trailed her warm fingers along his forearm.

Mira was a good cook and the food was delicious. He was grateful. He wasn't perfect and Mira wasn't perfect either, but their little Christmas dinner was as good as it gets. They lifted their glasses and toasted each other's health. David felt relaxed and happy, caught by the warmth of the moment.

Outside the snow fell softly. All over Mariposa, families were tucking into their Christmas dinner, giving thanks for all their blessings. David, too, offered up a silent prayer of thanks.

Chapter 20

The office was closed on Boxing Day, so David slept in and just took it easy basking in the warm afterglow of the Christmas dinner. Mira had put aside leftovers from the dinner for him to eat.

The first day back to work he was nodding off in the warmth of the room. He shook himself awake to look up into the pale blue eyes of Mildred Lemon standing in front of his desk, wearing her brown wool coat and with her big, brown carpet bag slung over her shoulder.

"I didn't want to disturb, you but I thought that this was important. I was cleaning out Cathy's desk, as Mrs. Proudfoot instructed. I thought you might be interested in this, a manila folder she kept there. It might be of some help."

"Thanks, Mildred, for dropping it off. I'll take a look at it while I have a cup of coffee."

"I do hope they catch her killer soon. People in this town are very nervous with a killer about, not knowing who he is. Please don't mention that I dropped in here. Mrs. Proudfoot would not like me poking my nose into things."

"Not a word. Your visit is just between you and me. We'll catch him, don't you worry, Mildred. I've got several good leads to go on. If you think of anything else feel free to drop by any time."

"That's reassuring news." With that, Mildred retreated.

David picked up the manila folder and looked inside. There was just a single sheet of paper, a copy of Dave Thompson's resume. Thompson had been teaching at Chesley High School two years ago before he came to Mariposa High. Now why would she want to keep a copy of his resume? Oh well, I guess she forgot about it and just left a copy in her desk. Or was she doing him a favour by helping him with his resume, by typing it out?

119

Chapter 21

The Sunday morning service after Christmas, between Christmas and New Year's, was always sparsely attended. People were tired from the holidays, or away on vacation. It was the very loyal that made an appearance, usually the seniors. Reverend Billy Day in his ankle length, white clerical robes, crossed in front of the altar and ascended into the pulpit to begin his sermon. Miss Temple, sitting directly below the pulpit in a pew, looked down at her watch pinned to her dress and noted the time. She hoped he'd keep his sermon short.

"The New Year is a new beginning, a time to put the past behind us. The New Year is a time to heal our pain, a time to reflect and a time to forgive. It is a time to reconcile ourselves with God.

"The past, the old year is gone forever. Some of our loved ones have departed. One of our young women was murdered. We cannot dwell on evil. We cannot let evil have the last word. We cannot undo the things we should have done or regret what we ought to have done. The past is the past. We must go forth and make this day the first day in our lives. Amen."

Miss Temple peeked at her watch. Reverend Day's sermon had taken just twenty minutes, not a minute over. It was a good beginning for the New Year.

After the benediction, Reverend Day stood by the front door shaking hands and greeting members who wanted to slip out without having coffee downstairs. Miss Temple didn't want to share any idle chitchat with Reverend Day or to compliment him on his sermon.

Instead she slipped down a side aisle leading to the church's gymnasium in the basement. Grabbing the banister, she carefully placed her feet on the carpeted stairs. At her age, a fall and a broken hip would be a death sentence.

George, with a hang dog expression, was leaning against the wall by the gym door.

"Morning, George."

George nodded.

Miss Temple quickly spied the refreshment table. It was set up in its usual place below the basketball. Two silver urns, one at each end and a cafeteria tray containing an opened carton of milk, a large bowl of sugar cubs and brown plastic stirrers had been placed on plastic doilies.

At another table, young children clutching their artwork were pushing and shoving to get their hands on plastic glasses of fresh lemonade. Miss Temple spied the homemade oatmeal cookies and made for them, taking two before the children ate them all. She next got into line at the tea urn.

Looking out at the crowd milling around, she hoped that some kind person would invite her in for Sunday dinner. She regretted her quick rejection of the Sandy's offer of Christmas dinner. How true, pride goeth before a fall. Now New Year's was coming up and she had no place to go.

She was really alone, an outsider, but she didn't want to be thought of as some poor old dear, someone to be nice to at this time of year. She didn't want to be critical of Reverend Day, but really he was so patronising. He only meant to be kind, but all those wet, slobbering kisses on her forehead and his 'dear Miss Temple' made her want to just spit.

She saw the ever formidable Miss Cassidy, the church's secretary talking animatedly with Mrs. Sandy. She placed herself behind them, hoping to overhear what they had to say.

"If you asked me who murdered that girl, I would finger George, the church janitor," said Mrs. Cassidy.

"Oh, no. Surely not. Why him?"

"I had asked him to put salt on the church steps at all the entrances. He did. All the ones, except the steps I use leading up to the church office. I almost killed myself when I stepped out for a breath of fresh air. I slipped on the icy step and wrenched my back. George's carelessness almost killed me."

"Come now, Miss Cassidy, that wasn't intentional. He just forgot. It's a natural mistake. Oh, your poor back," clucked Mrs. Sandy, sympathetically, "back pain can be so hard on the nerves."

But Miss Cassidy wasn't to be soothed by sympathy. "I tried to get George to turn the heat up during the day. I'm freezing to death in my office. I can hardly move my fingers to type. What on earth was he up to when the thermometer dipped below zero? I hunted all over the church trying to find him. Finally I looked in the furnace room and there he was sitting in a corner, reading a dirty men's magazine with his eyes popping out of his head. He flushed beet red when he saw me and quickly shoved the magazine in between a pile of newspaper, hoping that I hadn't see what he'd been reading. A zebra never changes its stripes, nor does George. A member of the OPP came to have a chat with him recently. George is the one as far as I'm concerned."

Mrs. Sandy smiled patiently as if Miss Cassidy needed a great deal of understanding. "My dear, you can't judge a man capable of murder just because he absentmindedly forgot to place sand and salt on the office's icy steps and to turn the thermostat up. That's too extreme."

Miss Cassidy lowered her voice and whispered, "I could tell you a lot more, but it's confidential. All I will say is once a bad apple, always a bad apple."

"Obviously, you don't believe a person can change for the better."

"For some," said Miss Cassidy, looking around to make sure she wasn't overheard, 'some'. As for that sweet old lady, Miss Temple, do you see her around?"

"Not at the moment."

"She's been defacing our hymn books." Miss Cassidy arched her eyebrows.

"Really!"

"Yes, my dear. She takes out her pen and makes changes. I've seen her do it quite a few times. If she does it again and I catch her, Miss Temple will go blind before her time."

"Oh, no," laughed Mrs. Sandy, "you can't be serious. We all know that you wouldn't do that. We know that you have a heart of gold."

"Some heart, some gold," said Miss Cassidy, under her breath, "just watch me."

Overhearing her name maligned in such a dreadful manner, Miss Temple quickly walked away. She went and stood by the refreshment table again. She hoped that by standing there in this busy area, someone would come up and talk to her.

Gale Chirp came up to refill her cup.

"You're looking very pretty this morning, my dear. That scarf around your neck is very becoming. It goes with the colour of your eyes," Miss Temple peered a little closer," green, aren't they?"

"Oh, Miss Temple. I'm so happy," said Gale. "I want to tell you a secret because I know you can keep it. Later, I will tell the world and shout it from the roof tops. I love Reverend Day and I think it's mutual."

"Oh, my dear, this is news," said Miss Temple hugging herself with joy at this scandalous piece of information.

"Er...but what about his wife?" blushed Miss Temple.

Gale pretended not to hear and waving at someone across the room, left to speak to them.

Miss Temple couldn't believe what she'd just been told. What about Mabel? Where does she fit into all this? Happiness is so elusive. Like quicksilver, sometimes it just slips through the fingers, like... sugar. She hoped that Gale was not suffering from false delusions and had inflated ideas over a compliment, or a few well-chosen words. Women can get carried away very quickly. But the main question was, where did Mabel fit in?

Miss Temple gave a start. Dr. Sandy, standing in front of her was asking, "Miss Temple, How's my favourite patient to-day? You seem to be far away. Day dreaming, Miss Temple?"

"No, just thinking. I'm very well, thank you, considering my age."

"Miss Temple, you will outlive us all. All those nice elderly ladies like yourself, with weak fluttering hearts, live to be a hundred, while the rest of us, like me, drop off like flies."

"Really," said Miss Temple, taking a good look at Dr. Sandy, surely he wouldn't drop dead in front of her with a heart attack. But one never knew. Count one's blessings while one can. Miss Temple decided to share her new secret with Dr. Sandy, the soul of discretion. "Gale, the church soloist," and she nodded in her direction, "has just told me something strange. She has fallen in love with Reverend Day and she feels the emotion is mutual. Is there any truth in it? What about Mabel?"

"What about her? Where is she, by the way?" said Dr. Sandy, glancing around.

"She's sitting over there, talking to a friend. She appears so calm. Do you think she knows about this?"

"Whether she does or doesn't, I don't think it's a wise idea for us to get involved. Alexander the Great used to shoot, with an arrow, the messenger who brought him bad news. Let's leave it at that."

Dr Sandy's answer was not the response she wanted. Miss Temple liked to sift and sort out the 'whys' and 'what ifs' and mull over each gossipy little detail with a sympathetic listener. She hadn't expected the subject to be dropped like a stone. That explained why Reverend Day's car was parked so often outside the Chirp House. How naive she'd been to think it was Mabel who'd been doing the visiting. It had been Reverend Day. What a hypocrite. She smiled to herself. Wait until the congregation gets wind of this. Then the fireworks will begin. She was excited by the idea. Nothing like a scandal to start the New Year off right.

Chapter 22

Dr. Sandy's doorbell rang

"Don't get up, Hal, I'll get it. You just sit there, put up your feet and relax. You've had a hard day," said Mrs. Sandy. "I hope it not another patient who desperately wants to see you. Whatever the emergency is, it will have to wait."

When she opened the door, she found George, the church janitor, standing there slouched in his black overcoat, his rumpled hat held pathetically in his hands.

"Come in, come in my good man. Don't stand there in the cold. Take your overcoat off. Sit here by the fire and warm yourself."

George slumped down in a big overstuffed chair putting out his feet close to the fire.

"Has the church caught fire? I hope it's nothing serious, George."

"Mrs. Sandy, I apologise for intruding on you like this. I feel embarrassed, but it's something I have to speak to your husband about. I need your husband's help."

"Yes, yes, of course, George," said Mrs. Sandy. "I'll go and get my him. Meanwhile I'll make us some nice hot tea."

In black lounge trousers, a V-neck Polo sweater, and loafers, the tall figure of Dr. Sandy came downstairs. Coming into the room, he pushed his spectacles up, so that they were resting on his forehead. "This is unexpected, George, what brings you here in this kind of weather? It's rather cold to be out and about."

"Um, yes. You see, I need your help urgently or I will lose my job. They're trying to pin Cathy Snifton's murder on me."

"Why you?" said Dr. Sandy looking at George very hard.

"When that girl was murdered, the cops checked out anyone with a record." George sighed. "I can't hide. I've got a record, a prison record. I've done time. That cop doing the investigation he came around to my place when I wasn't home. My landlady let him have a look around." George looked embarrassed and wished that the floor could swallow him up.

125

He could hardly look the doctor in the eye.

"Go on."

"You see, I had a large collection of porno magazines."

"So?" said Dr. Sandy smiling, "A lot of men have collections of this sort, George. It's normal. You can't go to jail for having a magazine collection. But that isn't the problem, is it?"

"No, Sir, it's much more serious than that. You're going to find out sooner or later so I might as well tell you. I will tell you everything. You see, my wife, she didn't die of natural causes. That's what I told everybody. I killed her one night when we both had been drinking heavily all day. We were both alcoholics. She was pretty mean when she was drunk, used to say some pretty nasty things. I had a complete blackout that night. When I woke up in the hospital afterwards they told me what I had done. I had stabbed her to death with a butcher knife and then had tried to hang myself, but the rope broke. I was even unlucky in killing myself.

"I couldn't believe that I had done such a thing. I got ten years for manslaughter. I served two thirds of my sentence and got out early on good behaviour. I was put on probation. The conditions for parole were that I held a job and attended A.A. meetings. What am I going to do? What is going to happen to me? They're out to get me. How am I going to defend myself? Who will believe me? You don't know how bad I felt about what I'd done, how many times I regretted it. The only explanation for that awful night is that my wife might have triggered it. We never got along. We used to fight a lot. She was always bugging me, saying that I wasn't man enough for her. Then she'd get mean and slap me around. I was brought up to never raise a hand to a woman, but she must have pushed me over the edge that night. I will regret it to my dying day, even though I can't remember it at all. But now there's this murder of a young girl, you know, the one that sings in the church choir. The cops have been snooping around because I've got a record. They're going to try and pin it on me. They can't find anyone else, then they'll decide it was me. What am I going to do?"

Dr. Sandy got up and stood warming his hands in front of the fire. George's story reminded him of when he was out hunting and heard the cries of a mother raccoon struggling desperately to free its tiny feet caught in the jaws of a bear leg trap. Without any hesitation, he had bent over to open the iron jaws of the trap to free the petrified animal

"I believe you, George," said Dr. Sandy, walking away from the fire to stand by George's chair. "Buck up. If you say you're innocent, then you are. God will see to that. What you need is to have someone to talk to, someone to give you emotional support. What about Reverend Day, our minister?"

George gave him a strange look. "He's only interested in women's problems. He'd be no help with mine. I find him difficult to talk to."

"I see," said Dr. Sandy, "George, give me time to think about it in the next couple of days and then phone me again."

Carrying a tray, Mrs. Sandy re-entered the room. "I see you've had your little chat, and now for some nice hot tea."

"Thank you kindly, Mrs. Sandy," said George.

When George had gone, Mrs. Sandy turned to her husband, "That poor man. Can't we do anything? He can't possibly have anything to do with that girl's murder."

"Mm, you're right, my dear. He's probably innocent. But it's not up to us to meddle. It's a matter for the police."

"Oh, Hal, I do wish we could remember something that could be helpful."

"I'm trying to do my best, dear. Quite a few young women get pregnant, but rarely do they get murdered."

Chapter 23

The sky was a bright blue, the sun was shining and the snow had stopped falling.

David poked his head around the office door, "Happy New Year, Clancy, baby."

"My, my, you're in a good mood today. You must've got lucky. What's your New Year's Resolution?" asked Clancy. "Is it to chase wild women?"

David laughed, "You know as well as I do. New Year's resolutions only get made to be broken. Besides, it's too cold out there to do much chasing."

"Cold weather never stopped anyone," laughed Clancy. "How did you celebrate New Year's? Did someone make a move on you?" Clancy was hoping for some salacious details.

"Fuck you. I drank beer and looked at the Rose Bowl game on TV. Now does that satisfy you? I come in this morning, bright-eyed and bushy-tailed ready to accomplish great things and you're giving me a hard time."

"Only the young and restless are in a good mood after the holidays," commented Clancy with a raised eyebrow. "Look at Greg over there. He looks knackered, hardly able to pull his socks up and tie his shoe laces. We'll be lucky to get anything done with him in that condition."

David went to his desk and checked the time, 9:05. School was in after the holidays. Now would be a good time to get hold of Bob Thompson. He had tried several times to contact him at home over the holidays but only got his answering machine. He was probably away. He picked up the phone. Everyone in Mariposa must be calling the High School that morning. It took him two attempts before he heard a click, then the crisp, efficient voice of the secretary saying, "Mariposa High. How can I help you?"

"I want to get hold of Bob Thompson."

"Please hold while I check his home room and timetable."

In the background David could hear the high school

orchestra playing a very faltering version of 'O Canada' over the P.A. system. There were a couple of lines in French, even he didn't know the words. What a country, half the population didn't know the correct version of the national anthem.

Mr. Stanley, the principal, cleared his throat, then proceeded with the day's announcements. "Welcome back from the holidays. I know everyone will want to settle right down and do serious work."

The school secretary came back on the line. "According to our timetable, Mr. Thompson doesn't have a spare until eleven o'clock. Can he get back to you then? If you leave your name and number, I'll tell him that you called."

She was as good as her word. Promptly at eleven a.m., Thompson returned the call.

"I got your message. What is this about? A student?" He sounded cautious.

"No, it's about someone you knew, the murdered librarian, Cathy Snifton."

"Oh."

David could hear the gasp in his voice. "When is a mutually convenient time for us to get together? I want to know what you know about her."

"How about fifteen minutes from now? There's a coffee shop, Manny's Grill, several blocks from the school. There won't be anyone in there at this time of day."

Manny's Grill, a greasy spoon that sold hot dogs, hamburgers and french fries to the Mariposa High school students, who'd rather eat there than in the school cafeteria, was deserted.

David walked in the door, past the silent juke box and the three pinball machines against the wall, to the back. The owner grey haired Manny Kovacs, in shirt sleeves and apron, was sweeping the floor.

At the far end of the counter, a fair haired man in his late twenties, approximately six feet tall, and wearing a black leather jacket, got up from the counter stool and held out his hand. "Bob Thompson."

Clean cut, ordinary and nondescript, thought David appraising Bob closely, a typical teacher.

"Where can we sit and talk?"

"In the back. Don't worry about Manny. He's got a hearing loss from all the noise generated by the pinball machines."

If Thompson was apprehensive about being questioned, he didn't show it. He appeared poised and self-confident, but then he'd have to be, coping with the kinds of kids they had to teach these days.

"Tell me about Cathy Snifton?"

"Why are you asking me? Plenty of people knew her."

"I'm asking you, because you went out with her for several months and you might know her better than a lot of people. That's why."

"What do you want to know? She was part of the Friday night crowd. I liked to talk to her because she liked to talk about the same things I did. We both liked the outdoor life, downhill and cross-country skiing, canoeing in summer, bicycling."

"How long did you go out with her?"

"A couple of times. More off than on."

"When?"

"Several months ago. She wanted me to spend more time with her, to be her boyfriend and I just wanted to keep it casual. I was straight with her and I told her."

"Where did you go on dates?"

"Sometimes we'd take in a movie, but that had its limitations. There is, as you know, only one movie house in town. Some Saturdays we took off a few hours to do some cross-country skiing. It's beautiful north of here."

"When was the last time you were out with her?"

"Mm," Bob paused, "It might have been the end of November."

David detected a tightness around the eyes, a certain wariness or was it just his imagination?

"A copy of your resume was found in a folder she kept in her desk. Why did she have it?" He leaned forward to catch Thompson's answer.

"She volunteered to type up my resume for me. That's all. She said she liked to type and it was no problem. She told me that she'd do it in her spare time."

"Why did you want it typed? Were you considering changing jobs? When was this?"

"October. I'd been teaching here for three years and I thought I needed a change. She offered and I accepted. It was no big deal." A slight flush came over Bob's face. There's something more to this, thought David.

"So that was all it was. Why would she keep a copy for herself? What was the point of that?"

"Search me. She was doing me a favour and probably typed it up at the library and just left a copy in her desk."

"Where were you on Friday, December the thirteenth?"

"I was out of town, attending a OSSTF conference down in Toronto at the Sheraton Hotel. I spent the evening with some other teaching friends, a couple who live in the Beaches."

"Their names?"

"Certainly, Tim and Celia Blake. They live on Bracken Avenue."

"When is a good time to reach them?"

"Supper. They don't eat out much."

"You were in their company all evening?"

"Yes. They will verify that." Thompson looked at his watch. "I've got to get back to class."

"Sure." David followed him out of the shop.

David went back to his desk and pulled out Bob Thompson's resume from the drawer. There is something here that's embarrassing to Bob Thompson, something I'm missing. Curious, and acting on a hunch, he decided to phone his previous employer at Chesley High and see what they had to say.

He asked to be put through to the Principal. After a few minutes of talking to Mr. Hunter's secretary, Mr. Hunter came on the line. David identified himself and the reason for his call, working on a murder inquiry here in Mariposa. "I'm trying to get a handle on Bob Thompson, a teacher who taught at your school several years ago."

"What's he done?" was the quick retort.

David was surprised at his reaction. "Nothing so far. Just want to ask a few questions. We had a recent murder here, a young woman. I am trying to build up a picture of what the murder victim was like. She had gone out with Dave Thompson and I found his resume in her desk. Curious, I decided to give you a

131

call."

"Is he one of your suspects?"

"At this point in my inquiry, I'm just checking things out."

"He was an excellent teacher."

"Did any incident happen at the school to cause him to change jobs? Why did he leave? Did he give a reason for leaving?"

Mr. Hunter gave a long pause then said, "There was a reason. I'll get right to the point, since this phone call is confidential, is it not? Thompson was a good teacher and I had no problem with him. But he left here under a cloud. It probably has very little to do with what you are investigating."

"Let me be the judge of that."

"There was an incident that happened before he left. A teenage girl stayed in his classroom after school, asking for help with her homework. She accused him of sexual assault. He denied it, but her parents raised a stink. They believed their daughter. They wouldn't drop the matter and I thought it would be wise for him if he moved on. It was a case of he said, she said. The case had no substantiation, no witnesses. The girl was a bit of a truant and was known to lie. Probably her reason was that she got home late after meeting her boyfriend and had to come up with a story. Every time she was questioned she changed her story. I gave him a good reference and he found another teaching job, I believe at Mariposa High School in Mariposa. Is that helpful? Has there been any problem?"

"No, none, just making inquiries. The victim had his resume in her work desk and I'm trying to find out why."

"No idea," said Mr. Hunter, "I take a teacher's word against a student any day. Kids will lie to your face. Bob was a good conscientious teacher, dedicated to his job and I have no trouble in recommending him."

"Thank you. I appreciate that. Sorry to have troubled you, Sir." David rang off.

Very Interesting. Other than typing out the resume as a favour, what other use what other reason would Cathy have for this resume? She kept it for some reason. What if she found out this information too? She might have used it to blackmail him.

But what did she want from him in return? I will have to ask him.

*****

Around supper time, when he figured the Blakes would be home, he phoned to check out Thompson's alibi.

A young woman's voice answered.

He asked, "Is this Celia Blake?"

"Speaking. Can I help you?"

"It's about Bob Thompson, I'm eliminating suspects in a murder that we have had up here in Mariposa. He supplied the names of husband and you as alibis. It was for Friday, December the thirteenth. Can you remember that date and what you did?"

"No problem. Dave drove down from Mariposa after school for an OSSTF meeting. We had supper when he got here around seven p.m. and then went to the Sheraton Hotel for the meeting. He was in our company the whole time. He stayed with us overnight and then went back to Mariposa the following day. Is that what you want to know?"

"Yes, thank you."

Well this information puts Thompson out of the picture for Friday, the thirteenth. Or does it?

Chapter 24

Another overcast day with grey snow clouds in the sky and the snow pelting down. Mabel felt terribly depressed, standing at the kitchen sink looking out of her window across the garden at the huge snow drifts piling up. The darkness of the winter months, like the greyness of this winter morning, seemed to stretch endlessly. It was so hard to get up in the morning. She had nothing to look forward to. She returned to the table, bringing with her the glass coffee percolator from the stove. She poured Billy another cup.

Billy stopped reading his newspaper to look at his coffee cup. "How many times have I told you, Mabel, that we'll get food poisoning from a cracked cup. I'll have to throw out that cup myself."

"It was my mother's," protested Mabel, "I can't bear to throw it out."

"Put it up on a ledge to look at," said Billy, "but don't put it on the table again. What is this?" said Billy querulously holding up a bowl of bran. "Is this hamster food?"

"No, dear, it's fibre. It will keep you regular," joshed Mabel trying to make a joke of the situation. "It's good for your bowels."

"So kind of you, my dear," murmured Billy, "to think of my bowels."

Mornings were not her husband's best times, thought Mabel. But, of late, when were his best times? Billy kept his head stuck in a book, like a turtle in sand.

"Anything you care to comment on? Anything interesting you want to tell me that's in the news?"

Billy just grunted.

Mabel sat down opposite him, smoothing out the plastic covered tablecloth as she did so. "Billy, I have something to tell you. The weather is getting me down. Ever since that girl was murdered, I feel there's something ominous hanging over our heads. The police haven't caught the killer, have they? Have you heard anything at all? The papers say so little."

"Nothing," said Billy absentmindedly, "the police think it's someone she knew. We're all suspects, Mabel, you and me included, according to Dave Scott."

"I think I have a migraine coming on."

"Oh, not another one, Mabel. You should get out in the fresh air. Why don't you pay a social call on Miss Temple? She's lonely. She'd appreciate your company."

"The old lady who has all those cats living with her?"

"That's the one," said Billy. "Before Christmas she told me someone strangled her favourite cat."

He's more interested in that crazy old lady than he is in me, thought Mabel. She jumped up from the kitchen table, hurried down the hall and put on her coat.

"Where are you going, Mabel?" remonstrated Billy, "what about my boiled egg?"

"I need some fresh air," said Mabel, "you suggested that I visit Miss Temple, so I'm going there now."

"Be sensible. It's too early. The old lady might not be up."

"I can't do everything. Your egg will have to wait until supper." Mabel shut the door firmly behind her.

*****

Miss Temple didn't answer the first several rings. Then she finally came to the door in her housecoat and slippers.

"Mabel, what a surprise to see you so early in the morning. Do you realize it is only 8:30 a.m."

"Oh, is it? I hadn't realized," said Mabel,

"Well, don't just stand there, come in," said Miss Temple. "Would you like to borrow something, an egg, a cup of sugar, a cup of flour? If you do, I have to say no. I'm right out of everything. But not to worry. Come into the living room for a chat and a cup of coffee. It isn't often that the minister's wife pays a social call at this hour of the morning. Is everything alright?" asked Miss Temple. secretly hoping that everything wasn't.

"Please, Miss Temple. I didn't come to borrow anything. This is a sympathy call."

"For whom? I don't quite follow."

"For your cat. I heard that your cat had been strangled."

"Yes, yes, my dear, but that was several weeks ago."

"Oh," said Mabel looking around at the lace doilies on the tiny tables and at the spindly fragile chairs. Where could she safely sit? Some of the chairs were still covered in plastic sheets. The lamp shades still had their protective cellophane wrappings on them. A large white and orange striped cat sat blinking on a lovely Queen Anne chair. Another cat stretched out lazily atop a bookcase licking its paws. A third was rubbing its head against the dining room door. Mabel recognized the wallpaper design as that of William Morris, but it was faded and worn. Mabel was sure that when she'd entered the hall she'd smelled cat urine. The old lady probably didn't notice the smell, she was used to it. Nauseating. Tiny bowls of cat food and water had been placed on a newspaper in front of the sofa. Mabel almost stepped into one as she stumbled and fell into a chair covered in cat hair.

"Excuse me, Mabel, but that's Dief's favourite chair. Even though he's no longer with us, I can't bear to have anyone sit there."

Mabel shifted to another chair but not before sweeping the hairs off with her hands. "Have you thought of getting your cats spayed? That's what most sensible people do."

Miss Temple's pupils narrowed. "I want them to be like God intended, not altered or neutered by life or by man. Would you want to be fixed?"

What an insulting question, thought Mabel. There's no dignified reply to that. What a crazy old lady. As for the dead cat, Mabel didn't feel one ounce of sympathy for it. One cat less. What did it matter in the general scheme of things? As far as she was concerned, the fewer cats the better.

"Here's your coffee, Mabel."

"Thank you."

"I always liked your house, Mabel. It's so much bigger and grander than my tiny cottage. Is it warm in winter?"

"It can be drafty at times."

"Your husband is always so busy. Do you think he's working too hard? Is he getting a good night's sleep?"

Mabel looked sharply at Miss Temple. Was that an innocent question, or was there something behind that comment? Miss Temple's face gave nothing away. Her calm and

136

serene countenance stared blankly back at her.

"The work of the church must be so exhausting," bubbled Miss Temple. "The choir sings such beautiful anthems, don't you think? Wasn't that a lovely solo that Gale Chirp gave last Sunday? She sings with an inner glow, don't you think, Mabel? I have never seen her so happy lately. Do you think Gale is in love?" Miss Temple regarded her with hooded eyes.

Mabel stared at her. That sly old bitch. What is she trying to tell me? Do I have to sit here and be insulted? Mabel felt she was suffocating in this horrid little room. She had to get away. She put her cup down on the table, got to her feet and reached for her coat.

"I have to go."

"But my dear, you haven't finished your coffee," protested Miss Temple rushing after her, "and I haven't finished my story."

"Goodbye," said Mabel firmly, opening the door.

"Do come again," said Miss Temple

Mabel trudged home to their big, creaky, old house, with its drafts under the doors and the windows. It cost a fortune to heat it in the winter. She took off her scarf and coat then paused to look at herself in the hall mirror. Dull and drab was what she saw. Salt and pepper streaked hair, a double chin, thickened waist, thick ankles She was a middle-aged matron. The more she looked the smaller she seemed to become in the mirror. She felt like a handy-mop, a Swiffer broom, a Tupperware brush,

Last night, as on many previous nights, she couldn't get to sleep. She was alone in a big empty house. The grandfather clock in the downstairs hall had chimed away the hours as she tossed and turned, rolled this way and that, waiting for Billy to come home. The wind howled outside and the house creaked and groaned inside, almost if there was a ghost hovering in the attic. She was alone. It was not good to be alone. She looked at the clock on the small table beside her. One a.m. Had Billy been in an accident on those icy roads? Was that why he wasn't home? She could think of all sorts of accidents that could have happened, like falling on ice, tripping on steps, twisting an ankle. So many things could go wrong in the middle of the night.

Finally, she heard the key in the front door lock, the door

creak open, then close, footsteps along the hall floor. The creaking of footsteps on the stairs. Then Billy was standing beside the bed. She looked at him, his hair rumpled, a button missing on the front of his white shirt, his buckle undone on his belt. He was carrying his shoes so as not to awaken her.

"Where have you been, Billy? It's so late. I've been worried sick about you. I lie here and imagine all sorts of things have happened to you."

Billy sighed. "Oh, Mabel. I've been doing the work of the Lord. The prayer meeting ran late. Someone had a birthday which we celebrated. We had coffee and cake afterwards which took up some time. Go back to sleep. Nothing to worry about."

Mabel lay back on the pillow, not able to close her eyes. She lay there in the darkness, hoping that sleep would come now that Billy was besides her, safe and sound. She was not alone in this old house.

Chapter. 25

These long winter nights were getting to David. He missed the soft, warm, comforting presence of his wife cuddling next to him. The window panes in his apartment were glazed with ice. At the end of the day he needed someone to come home to, to talk to, someone to share his day with. Being single again was no joy. It was a curse in this small town, everyone was either engaged, going steady or married. For Mira he felt a little guilty. He had not followed up on that lovely Christmas dinner. He had thanked her and he was grateful but he had made no promises, no commitments. Whatever void Mira felt, he could not fill it.

He thought wistfully about the beautiful Clara Clarke. You poor fool, she doesn't give a tinker's damn about you. She's in love with Tom Ball, the boy next door.

But several times a week before turning in for the evening, David found himself driving slowly along Brant Street, past Clara Clarke's cottage, just checking to see that everything was alright, that the coach light was on above her front door and the front walk had been cleared of snow. He had hoped that he might catch a glimpse of Clara at the windows, but all the blinds were drawn.

This time he stopped his car and walked up to the door. He rang the bell, hoping to find her alone. After a few minutes, he heard light footsteps in the hall and then the lock turned in the door.

"I'm glad you're got your door chain on, there's still a murderer loose. You can't be too careful. Am I intruding?"

"Well," said Clara glancing down at her pink velour housecoat, "as you can see, I'm not exactly dressed for company." She covered her mouth as she yawned.

"My visit will be short. I have a big day ahead of me tomorrow, too." He followed her into the living room. Clara didn't ask him to take a seat so he remained standing.

"Has anyone been bothering you? Have you been getting any funny phone calls?"

"No, there haven't been any," replied Clara with a bored

voice. "Everything has been calm and peaceful around here."

"I noticed that you still have your Christmas tree up in the corner. Would you like my help in taking it down? I'm very handy around the house."

"After the Three Wise men come," said Clara, "then I'll take it down. How is your work going?"

"It's percolating...just like hot coffee." David hoped that she'd take the hint, but Clara chose to ignore it. No coffee for him.

He picked up a silver framed photograph of Clara standing with her parents in front of the house.

"My parents are both dead. It was taken three years ago. They were killed in a car crash."

"I'm sorry to hear that, Clara." Still looking at the photo, David said, "I hear that you have been keeping company around town with your next door neighbour, Tom Ball?"

"That's my own business. Is that a crime?"

David, stung by her rebuff, retorted, "You've always been in love with Tom, haven't you. You've always been in love with the boy next door."

"No," said Clara, softly, "that's not true." She blushed to the roots of her golden hair.

"Really," said David, letting her embarrassment speak for itself. "The way I see it, while Cathy was alive and dating Tom, you were out of the picture. Now that she's dead, Tom's up for grabs and you have a clear field. That gives you a very good motive for murder."

Clara's large, brown eyes welled up with tears. "You make it sound ugly which it isn't." Tears trickled down those beautiful high cheek bones.

"Here," said David gruffly, "I hate to see a woman cry," and he handed her his handkerchief. "Look, I'm not your enemy. I'm on your side. I just want to get at the truth."

"Do you really want the truth?" sobbed Clara. "Do you really think that I would, that I would cause another person's death?"

He reached out and put his hand gently on her shoulder.

"No," said David, "I believe that you had nothing to do with Cathy's death, but... Tom." David shrugged his shoulders, "that might be a different story." David wanted to say, 'Clara you're too good for Tom. You're wasting your time on him.' But he stopped short of doing so. No woman wants to be told that they're too good for a man. They have to come to that conclusion themselves.

"Look, I know you're confused and upset about all this. How about I leave you my home phone number. If you have any questions or just want to talk or discuss any problem, just call me."

"Thank you." Clara stood up and handed him back his handkerchief. "I don't know what to think or believe any more. The whole thing is giving me a splitting headache. I think I'll just go to bed now."

David excused himself, leaving behind a very unhappy Clara Clarke.

Chapter 26

The next day, David called and left a message at Mariposa High for Bob to meet him at 4 pm at Manny's Grill.

"Why do you want to see me again? Didn't my alibi hold up?"

"Yes, your friends vouched for you. I checked your work references. I phoned your former employer to get an idea of why Cathy Snifton kept your resume. Cathy Snifton knew about your past, didn't she? That was why she had your resume still in her desk."

Thompson's face went beet red. He paused then stammered, "I might as well tell you, the little bitch was trying to blackmail me about something. You'll find out anyhow, it will save you time and trouble. Cathy was trying to intimidate me over something. I wouldn't use the word blackmail. How shall I put it. I didn't trust her. I didn't know when or where she'd blurt out my secret."

"Please explain."

"A couple of weeks after she'd typed up my resume, we were both down at the bar. We both were feeling no pain. I had put away a few and then I playfully gave a light pat to the waitress on the buns. I apologized. The waitress wasn't bothered by it. But Cathy snidely blurted out, 'patting girls on the backside again!' Again? Her remark hit me like a thunderbolt. Where did that remark come from? Behind my back she had sneaked around and found out my history at my last school."

"Go on."

"I had left my last school under a cloud. A disturbed fifteen-year-old girl in my class, resentful because I had given her a failing grade, tried to blackmail me. She met me after class and said if I didn't pass her, she'd run and tell the principal that I had patted her on the breasts and buns. I told the little tramp I wouldn't. I should have protected myself by not being alone with her. She flew to the principal. The principal believed me, but we both felt that I should move on. Her parents were raising a stink. So I came here and there has been no problem with female students since."

"Were you surprised about Cathy's remark?"

"I couldn't believe my ears. She had gone snooping and ferreted out this information behind my back. I trusted her. Just a simple typing job, a resume, that she volunteered to do."

"You figured that she'd say it again, didn't you?"

"Yes, I figured that she'd blurt out my secret after a few too many drinks. I'm a teacher, a professional person, and to have this kind of rumour circulating around wouldn't help me. You can be sure of that."

"Was it so threatening to you that you decided to kill her?"

"Hell no. I was just going to leave at the end of the school year. I would just slip away. Hand in my resignation and apply to another school board. I would get good references from Mariposa High. I had nothing to do with her murder."

"You can't keep running. You can't keep changing schools and places."

Bob looked grim. "I know. I don't expect you to believe me. But I am telling you the truth."

*****

Back at the office, like the predictable town crier in the square, Clancy bellowed out, "Bob White has been looking for you. He dropped by to see how you were handling the Snifton murder case. He wanted to ask you how it was shaping up. He looks lean and mean. He had a hungry look. I don't think he ate much turkey over the holidays," Clancy laughed, patting his full stomach. He looked over at Greg, sitting in the corner happily munching on a maple sugared doughnut. Greg waved back at him a high five, no grief, no break and enter.

"Oh, here he comes now, cheers." Clancy made a dive into the paperwork piled up high on his desk.

After giving a short nod to Clancy, Bob White said to David, "Give me the goods on the Snifton murder case. How is it going? I tried to get over from Barrie, but you know how things are. It's been a zoo over the holidays."

David found it hard to hide his feelings, to keep his

antagonism out of his face. Same old snow job. The bullshit never changes. I do all the donkey work, get no thanks and then White arrives on the scene to collect the goodies, he gets the praise. But looking at it positively, maybe White can give me the benefit of his superior insight and experience.

"Let's hear it." demanded White.

"The victim was sexually active with several partners. At the time she was murdered, she was three months pregnant. Was the victim blackmailing her lover for money or marriage? Which one? My prime suspect is Ted Chirp, a married man now separated, known for his previous violent attacks on his wife. On the night Snifton was murdered, his story is that he dropped her at the park around 10:30 p.m. or earlier. He denies being the father of her unborn child. He doesn't deny being sexually involved with her. He says that she told him that she was pregnant and that he gave her some money to help pay for an abortion. Chirp wants to get back with his wife. If news of his involvement with Snifton got out and reached his wife's ears, it would make a reconciliation very difficult, almost impossible. He might have worried about being squeezed financially more than once by her. His motive: he murdered her to get her out of his life."

"A good bet. Who are the others?"

"Snifton had a long standing relationship with Tom Ball. He knew her from high school. Their history goes back a long way. His story is that he didn't know that she was in the park that night. Ball has a good motive and he was in the park near the time she was murdered. Snifton could have arranged to meet him there to blackmail him for money, or marriage, or both. His father, who owns Balls Haberdashery, has a bad heart condition. Scandal would kill him. Ball says that in the park he didn't hear or see anything unusual. He was just walking his dog. He has no alibi after 10:30 p.m."

"Alone, walking his dog on a Friday night, what a fairy story. Turn the heat up on that one."

"My third suspect is weak. Bob Thompson, a high school teacher, said he stopped seeing Snifton several months back. His story is that he spent the weekend in Toronto after he left the bar. I checked out his witnesses. They can vouch for him. I can't break the time frame. It would be impossible to get away for two hours. It takes two hours to drive to Toronto from there. He has an iron shut alibi.

"Then there is George Kerr the janitor at Mariposa United who is up on life probation for a manslaughter charge. He stabbed his wife to death in a drunken brawl. He has done his time, has a job, and is living in a rooming house. He has no alibi."

"Keep an eye on him. Try to find out if they have had any personal interaction. What motive would he have? Except his secret of having spent time in the pen. Not so promising. Keep him on the back burner, unless you get any further information to bring him forward. As for the other two, keep going over their stories. Keep going back to them, see if they change their stories in any way. Look for discrepancies and the reason why," said White, smiling at David. "You're doing a great job. I couldn't have done better myself."

"Thanks."

"As soon as I can, I hope to help you on this case, possibly in the next couple of weeks. I've got to head out now."

"Great," said David, but privately he wondered just when White was going to lift a finger. It's all excuses, excuses. Next week he'll have another excuse for not being here.

Chapter 27

"Time for a coffee break." Clancy got up from his desk and waddled over to the machine to pour himself a cup. He took a sip and then spat it out. "Crap. You lazy slob, Davy," he yelled. "Today, it's your turn to brew coffee. You let that coffee sit there for two days without brewing a fresh cup. Dump it out and go get us some fresh stuff. Really, Davy, caffeine makes you perky. Your brain needs a jolt."

"Look, I'll make a fresh pot." said David getting up from his desk. "And by way of an apology, I'll go get a coffee at Apple Annie's and bring it back to you,"

Clancy was too much sometimes.

Walking down Mississauga Street towards Apple Annie's, David spotted Mrs. Sandy, the doctor's wife, engaged in conversation with Miss Temple outside the hardware store probably still talking about cucumbers and naked males crapping on her front lawn. Miss Temple gave him a quick nod and scurried off.

"How's the investigation going?" asked Mrs. Sandy, giving him one of her bright smiles.

"Ongoing." Impulsively he asked, "Mrs. Sandy, it's time for a break. Care to join me for a cuppa? I need some fresh insight. Care to share your thoughts?"

"What a nice idea," said Mrs. Sandy. "It isn't often that a married woman like myself gets an offer like that. I was going into the hardware store to buy some wire for picture framing, but it can wait. You know, Mr. Scott, I have been going over and over in my mind what happened to Cathy, desperately trying to recall something that would be of help to you."

"Maybe you can. Cathy Snifton was one of your husband's patients, wasn't she?"

"Yes, she was."

David followed her into Apple Annie's and they took a seat at the back. He was very interested in hearing the answer to his question. When they got seated he asked, "Were you helping out in your husband's office the day Cathy got the news that she was three months pregnant?"

"Yes, Hal asked me over the intercom to bring in Cathy's file. Her lab result had just come in that day. I just help Hal out in the afternoons several days a week. I don't work full time. I know what this is leading up to," Mrs. Sandy smiled wisely, "you're going to ask me for information about one of Hal's patients which is confidential."

"But this is a murder investigation and the victim is dead."

"You're right. I don't believe that I'm violating Cathy's trust in assisting the police in finding her murderer. What I tell you is strictly confidential, part of what Hal related to me after she had left the office."

"Hold on a minute. Let me get two coffees. Milk and sugar?" asked David getting up from his chair.

"I take mine clear."

David returned with the coffees and sat down. "The police never reveal who told them what and it might help our investigation greatly," David assured her. "We all want to see justice done. I am interested in hearing Cathy's reaction to the lab result."

"At first, she thought the lab had made a mistake. She registered disbelief, 'This can't be.' Hal reiterated the result and asked if she wanted to take another test to confirm the result. No, she wouldn't take another test. Then she got angry. She slammed her fist down on the armchair, saying, 'This is just great!' Hal tried to help, show empathy. He told her that she had several options. She could choose to go full term and have the child adopted if she decided that she didn't want to keep it. Or, if she wanted to have an abortion, then she should have it as soon as possible. Hal wanted her to have the abortion within the next couple of days, a week at the latest. He explained to Cathy that she could take the day off work, come in at nine, have a d and c, which takes just half an hour, and then be back at work the next day with no one the wiser. No one needed to know. Her secret would be safe."

"What did she say to his suggestions?"

"She just sat there thinking, acting as if it were the end of the world. Hal suggested that if she wanted to keep the child, there were plenty of support networks for single mothers. A court order could get financial support from the father. When she still didn't say anything, Hal said, when you make up your mind, you can marry the father later, that is what some women do, have the child and marry later. That decision didn't have to be made then, now. To this Cathy replied sarcastically, 'Yeah, sure I will marry him later.' Then she burst into tears. She asked 'How can I keep the child?' and shook her head There was a desperate look in her eyes and then she asked again, 'How much time doctor have I got?'

"Hal said, 'One week to do it safely, if you put it off longer, it increases the risk to yourself.' I remember her saying, 'I have only one week and a decision that I will have to live with for the rest of my life. Life isn't fair.' Cathy was really in a state when she came out of the office. Hal felt that she wanted to keep the child. On the other hand, there were a lot of problems if she did. He tried to explain to her that there were counselling services and advice centres, where she could go and talk to someone. But she just shook him off, got her things together and left."

"Did she ever phone or contact your husband's office again?"

"Never. She was murdered several days later."

"Did she ever hint to you who the father was? Did she give you any idea?"

"No, none at all. But call it women's intuition, I had a strong feeling at the time that, whoever the father was, he had other commitments. He wasn't available. it was just a hunch. I have nothing to base it on, but I felt that Cathy's news wouldn't be good news to the father of her child. She felt, I believe, that he would not marry her."

"Do you think he was a married man?"

"Mm. I won't go that far. All I got was the feeling was that she couldn't marry her lover at that point in time. Maybe he wasn't in love with her, or it was an affair with complications."

"I appreciate your input, Mrs. Sandy. Women sometimes have far more insight into the affairs of the human heart than men."

"What a nice compliment! You've made my day. Now I've got to get to the hardware store and get some wiring for the picture before I forget. It was nice talking to you. Cheers, until we meet again."

That conversation shed more light on the situation. Cathy wasn't in love with the father of her child. It may have been an affair that went wrong, the inconvenience of a pregnancy that was going to interrupt her life and her plans to leave Mariposa, her plans for freedom. The father of the child could not or would not marry her.

Cathy blackmailed Bob Thompson. Who else did she blackmail? Keep asking questions until you get more answers.

Chapter 28

"The more I think about it, it's a tossup between Tom Ball and Ted Chirp." To vent his frustration, David used his elastic as a slingshot with a paperclip as a missile, and the target the wastepaper basket. So far he was missing the basket as the clips bounced off the wall.

Both these guys had the opportunity, both were in the park around the time Cathy was killed and both of them had a good motive, blackmail—Tom to get rid of her because he didn't want to marry her and Ted because he wanted to get back with his wife. "The more I interview them, the more I uncover. Bits and pieces keep bubbling to the surface. They don't change their story. They just leave out huge chunks of helpful information."

Getting up from his desk to stretch his legs, David decided to do several push-ups on the floor between the radiator and desk. Greg had gone out on a call and Clancy was on a break. He was on his tenth push-up when the clang of the fire engine leaving the station next door made the wooden floor tremble. David jumped up and reached for his jacket.

From his car, David could see the cloud of black smoke billowing upwards into the sky above the town. He followed the fire truck as it careened around the corners and headed for Simcoe Street. The Fire Truck and ambulance had screeched to a stop in front of the Muir House which was going up fast, with flames shooting out from the roof at the rear of the house, and great balls of thick smoke enveloping the roof.

By the time David parked his car, two firemen had jumped off the truck with axes and were running up the sidewalk to the front door, while two others were busy hooking up the hose to the yellow hydrant. Another was raising the aerial extension ladder to the windows of the second floor.

David looked up at the bedroom windows for signs of a shadow, or life of some kind. Mrs. Muir, who was bed ridden, wouldn't stand a chance of getting out, but James could get out. David hoped that for once James forgot about her and saved his own skin. If he lingered to rescue her, he was finished in this wooden frame house that was going up like kindling wood.

David glanced around at the growing crowd on the lawn. He spotted Mabel Day in her pathetically thin, black wool coat and winter boots, her teeth chattering and her hands dug into her coat pockets. He moved over to reassure her.

"They're doing the best they can, Ma'am."

"I know," Mabel, turned her anxious face towards him, "But will they be able to save them?"

"We can only hope. How did the fire get started?"

"I don't know and the fire marshal doesn't know either. It's a pokey old house. Faulty wiring may have caused it." David was puzzled by her pale face and twitching blue lips.

"James has been acting strange lately. He's been so depressed. He called on my husband the other night. I overheard them talking. I heard him say that the police were bugging him, asking him all kinds of questions about Cathy's murder. James said that they were like a dog that wouldn't let go of a bone. James has such a sensitive nature. He said that the questioning was getting him down. He said that he was very depressed and didn't think he could take much more of the questioning. Cathy's murder hit him hard."

"Depressed?"

"Guilt, I guess, from what he said to my husband. He said his conscience was troubling him."

"About what?"

"Cathy's murder, what else?"

David was surprised to say the least. "Did he say that? Did he confess to that? I don't have him in the park at the time she was murdered. He had an alibi. He felt guilty that he wasn't there to save her. That's what he felt guilty about."

"Oh, then I'm mistaken. I misheard. Forgive me. Forget that I even mentioned it."

"It might be wise, all things considered, to keep this opinion to yourself."

David left her to join Mrs. Sandy, who was standing on the edge of the crowd peering anxiously up at the house.

"Where's James? Why can't they find him?"

"The firemen are doing everything humanly possible. They'll find him."

"Alive, I hope."

David watched silently as hoses directed water onto the house, but the freezing air was quickly turning the water to ice. Large icicles dripped from the charred, broken windows, the eaves troughs and the veranda. Smoke clung to his clothes and seared his lungs.

The strong wind was blowing against the house fanning the flames even higher. He ducked around a ladder and went to stand by Tom Allen, the Fire Chief, who was busily directing his crew to hose different outbreaks of flames on the roof. David watched them anxiously. As soon as they put out one patch of flames, another patch would appear in a different spot.

"What's the chance of James getting out?"

"It depends," said Allen grimly. "If the water pressure holds and it doesn't freeze on us, the house stands a chance. Otherwise forget it. Timber goes up fast."

At the second floor, front window, a fireman's face suddenly appeared. He shouted down at them.

"We've found someone."

A minute passed, then a heavy, limp body was passed out through the window.

"It looks like Mrs. Muir," said David running over to the ladder.

"Yes, but she looks like a goner," said the chief. "She's not even moving. Look at the colour of her face." Mrs. Muir was placed on a stretcher and into the ambulance which sped away, its siren wailing.

"But where's James? Do you think James has a chance?"

At that moment, panting heavily, Mr. Neary came running across the lawn, breaking through the crowd of people. He ran over to David.

"When did the fire start?"

"About fifteen minutes ago, but the house is going up pretty fast."

"Did James get out in time? Have you seen him?"

"No, not yet."

"You mean he's still in there?" Neary took off sprinting through the crowds towards the front door with David following closely behind him. "You can't go in there. The smoke is too thick. You wouldn't stand a chance. You would be dead from carbon monoxide poisoning in minutes. Let the firemen do their job. They'll get him out."

"This is horrible...horrible. While I was at choir practice I noticed that James was absent. So afterwards, as soon as it was finished, I drove straight over. I thought that he might be sick or something. He's so good about phoning if he can't make it."

Another shout came from inside the building. They had found another body. "It must be James. It must be," shouted Mrs. Sandy.

James' limp body was carried down on the shoulders of a fireman.

"It is James.... Isn't it?" asked Mrs. Sandy rushing over to the stretcher to catch a glimpse of him. The ambulance attendants quickly wrapped his body in blankets and slapped an oxygen mask on his face. "He will live won't he?"

David said nothing. Neary ran over and walked with the attendants to the ambulance. He tried to jump in, but the doors were slammed in his face.

"I wish I could have been able to help. I wish I could have done something. I felt so helpless, standing here and doing nothing." A tear trickled down Mrs. Sandy's face. "I never thought it would come to this. It seems it's all too late."

"We are all too late, too late," echoed Mabel, her teeth chattering from the cold.

"Look," said David, "why don't you both go home and get warm. There's nothing that can be done here. The fire will be out soon. We can't do anything more. Go home, ladies."

"Come with me, Mabel," said Mrs. Sandy putting her arm around Mabel's shoulders. "I'm going your way. I'll walk you home."

Depressing, thought David after the fire had finally been put out and the crowd had dispersed. The four walls of the house stood in front of him, testament to that evening's tragedy.

In her white parka, Mira slipped out from behind a tree beside his car. There was a tightness in her face, tension around her mouth, a look which appeared to David to have nothing to do with the fire.

"Keeping busy?" asked Mira sharply.

"Hi, Mira. You surprised me standing there in the shadows. Were you here for the fire? Awful. wasn't it?"

"Yes. Are you too busy to see old friends?" The tone of her voice was crisp and cool.

"Mira, I'm on duty. My time isn't my time. I have a murder case to solve."

"I've heard that song before. Let me get out my violin. Too busy with work to phone, too busy with work to call. I thought we had something going."

Mira's eyes became pinpoints of blackness, "But not too busy to visit the school teacher, Clara what's her name. Is she a suspect in the murder case? Your evening discussions by the fireside must be very helpful."

David didn't answer. She made him feel guilty without his having done anything to feel guilty about.

"You're always busy, too busy to show or care whether I'm alive or dead."

"You're alive, Mira, very much alive."

"Thank heavens for that!" said Mira, "I need something to cheer me up. It's been a horrible night. It must be the weather, all this slush, mud and ice."

"The weather forecast is optimistic. Sunshine's promised for tomorrow. Keep your chin up."

"You don't suppose...?"

It would be so easy to hop into the sack with Mira, so easy to say yes, but his heart wasn't in it. "I can't Mira," the words were out of his mouth before he realized that he'd uttered them. Oh shit! Now you've gone and done it, he thought. There's nothing like the anger of a woman scorned.

"Well, if that's the way you feel about it. Around here there's no respect for the dead or the living. Take a hike." Mira leaving her sentence unfinished, turned on her heel and walked quickly to her car.

*****

The next morning, lying on David's desk was a telephone message from Barrie. 'Bob White's in a body cast for several months. There was a shoot-out in front of Canadian Tire when he'd stopped a suspect's car for speeding. The suspect had driven off while he radioed in the license plate. He'd taken out his gun but the suspect was faster. In the exchange, he got one bullet in the thigh and one in the groin.

"Did you like that nice message, I left?" Clancy was like a slobbering hound with a hangover. He had a big grin all over his face. "Too bad. What a nice guy for that to happen to."

"How sincere you are."

"Who? Me? Sincerity is my middle name. I heard about the fire last night. Mrs. Muir was DOA at the hospital, and James, was just barely conscious."

"I'll phone the hospital to find out what's happened."

"Let me know."

From the Mariposa General Hospital, David heard that early that morning, James Muir had succumbed to carbon monoxide poisoning. He had never fully regained consciousness. David put the phone down and sat in silence just listening to the sounds of the room, the clanking of the radiator and the creaking of the window pane. Next he phoned Mrs. Sandy, she should be told as one of his friends. "I'm sorry to give you the bad news. Your friend, James Muir, died this morning."

"Thank you for calling me," said Mrs. Sandy softly. "I heard the news from my husband, who'd been up at the hospital. I tried to tell you at the fire, that I felt this could have been prevented"

"What do you mean?"

"The other night, when I went over to sit with his mother, James met me in the hall. He looked really depressed, almost suicidal. I'd noticed that he'd been acting this way ever since Christmas. He told me that in the past six months, he had been losing weight and felt tired all the time. He had a cough that he couldn't shake. He told me that he'd gone and had blood tests done. The tests came back. James had AIDS. He told me that, with Cathy dead, I was the only real friend he had. He said that he didn't want to be a burden on anyone. He was very agitated and said that he didn't know what he was going to do. He said he was desperate.

"AIDs is not a death sentence, I told him. You just have to take medication and to take care of your health. Patients have been known to live ten years or more, some a natural lifespan. Buck up, I said. I hope he didn't set the fire."

"I hope he wasn't driven to that," said David slowly. "We'll have to wait for Chief Allen's report. Then we'll know for sure."

*****

Two days later, the phone rang just as David was going through all the evidence trying to make a connection. What a mess. It was Tom Allen. Except when there was a fire when he had to be serious, he was slap-happy. It got on David's nerves. It was too early to be slap-happy.

"What is it?" asked David, crossly.

"Oh, my, aren't we civil today. I thought you would want to be the first to know that the Muir house had been torched. Arson, my friend. Someone set fire to the Muir house."

"Uh huh."

"You don't sound surprised."

"Go on. How was it done?"

"Gas chromatograph tests show that gasoline, a hydrocarbon with low molecular weight was splashed around the back of the house, possibly from a gasoline can. We didn't, though, find the can or container. Upstairs, Mrs. Muir was sleeping in her bedroom. James probably could have gotten out, but he stayed behind to rescue her. We found him on the floor next to her bed. Mrs. Muir was dead on arrival at Mariposa General. They both died from carbon monoxide poisoning from smoke inhalation, a common cause of death in a fire."

"Do you think that James set the fire deliberately, then had second thoughts about killing himself and his mother?"

"I thought of that possibility. But we found no traces of gasoline upstairs, near where we found James. No splashes on his clothing, on his skin, or on the floorboards underneath the body, or in the bedroom. My educated guess is, no. There would be some indication on the body, burn marks, splashes of gasoline. We could find nothing. A gasoline fire goes up pretty fast. Where was the container? He wouldn't have had time to get rid of it. It would have been found somewhere in the house. We

156

could find nothing."

"Do you have any idea who set it?"

"A firebug, who else? A person in the crowd who gets his jollies by seeing a building go up in flames. Sometimes in the crowd you can spot them, sometimes you can't. You were there. Did you notice anyone acting odd? Acting agitated?"

"Not off-hand. I was too busy trying to prevent would be rescuers from entering the house. But I'll work on it."

"A word to the wise, a firebug, if not caught, will light more. Catch him before he lights another."

After he put the phone down, David wondered why anyone would set fire to the Muir house. He mulled it. Who would want to kill the Muirs, a bedridden old lady and her son? Was the attack directed at James? Had James passed his disease on to someone else? That idea was farfetched. According to reports, James had only one lover, Neary, the church organist and there was no motive for him to torch the house. Nothing made any sense.

*****

"Mr. Miller, the funeral director is on the line for you," called out Clancy.

David picked up the phone

"I've got a problem, Constable. Scott. I saw you at the fire and, how can I put this, I was supposed to handle the funeral arrangements for the Muirs. But the hospital has informed me that James Muir had AIDs. I can't take the risk, nor can my employees, to deal with this. I'm too small an organisation, the extra costs for special gowns, gloves, etc., not to mention spillage and drainage. We can't do embalming."

"Where do I come in? What do you want from me?" asked David.

"Nothing really. It's just a suggestion. The Muirs could have a cheap simple graveside interment with Reverend Day saying a few prayers and a memorial service later, or just simply cremation with no viewing of the body. I imagine the family, whoever there is, will want the situation to be handled as discretely as possible."

"Of course."

The Muirs had no next of kin. David didn't think it would be much of a problem. He decided to do his good deed for the day and go and speak to Reverend Day. Before he got to the church, he spotted Day at the next traffic light, jogging up and down on the spot, waiting for the light to turn green.

"Can I have a word with you? We need your help. Mr. Miller, the funeral director, called me. He's suggested a simple graveside service. James can be buried without a service, but we, that is Mrs. Sandy and myself, thought it would be nice to have one. For health considerations, Mr. Miller has refused to do any embalming. That's his decision and we can't argue with it."

"Sure, no problem, I'll be glad to help."

"Your wife," said David, changing the subject, "I was speaking to her at the fire. She told me that she thought James had been involved in Cathy's murder and that, because of remorse, James decided to end his life, killing himself and his mother. Where would Mabel get an idea like that?" asked David.

Day smiled and shook his head. "My wife has a vivid imagination. She must have overheard our conversation. James visited me at home. He was very depressed and upset. My wife had probably caught snatches of our conversation. James told me that he felt a great deal of guilt about Cathy's death. I don't know why. But that's what he said," Day sighed. "I don't know why Mabel would want to make such idle speculation. She sometimes gets an idea fixed in her head."

"Interesting," said David.

Day shivered, "I've got to get going. I'm getting cold standing here."

"Of course," said David, and he pulled away from the curb as the light turned green.

*****

It's time for a little payback, a little justice thought David as he drove into the Mariposa United Church parking lot. Eager Miss Cassidy bobbed her head out of the office door, "Can I help you?"

"No, thank you, I'm here to see Mr. Neary."

"His office is just down the hall from Reverend Day's."

David knocked.

"Come in."

The room was in gloom. Neary hadn't bothered to turn on a light. He was sitting at his desk, reading sheet music. David didn't expect to see such a radical change in Neary's appearance. His face was ashen, his eyes bloodshot. Neary looked at David with dead eyes.

"Oh, it's you again."

"Yeah, it's me. Do you want to hear how the fire was started? It was arson."

"Arson! Who would want to do a thing like that?"

"That's what I want to find out."

"If you think I set it, think again, I was at choir practice. James was my special friend."

"No," said David, "I don't think you set it."

"Well then, why the visit?"

"This is a murder investigation. James died at the hands of an arsonist, but James himself did not have longevity in his system—ten years if he was lucky, two years if he wasn't."

"What do you mean?"

"James had s secret, didn't he Neary? Didn't he tell you his secret? You were his lover and best friend."

"I don't know what you're talking about," protested Neary.

"Yes, you do. James had AIDS. Yes, you do." He watched Neary turn beet red. "James had AIDS. He had all the symptoms; swollen glands, weight loss. He was terrified that if he told anyone he would be ostracised in this small town. I wonder who gave it to him? Was it James' one and only lover? I wonder if his lover, knowing that he himself carried the virus, continued to have sex with James without telling him, without being honest with him, without levelling with him, and giving James the option to choose between life and death. His lover was too selfish to practice safe sex."

"I don't know what you're driving at?"

"You know what I'm getting at. You were his lover and you continued to have sex with James, not giving a damn whether he caught the disease or not. You didn't use a condom. You committed murder as far as I'm concerned."

"Are you suggesting?" Neary's voice wavered, his Adam's apple bobbing in his throat, "that I killed James?"

"I'm suggesting that Mariposa is a small town. Mr. Miller, the funeral director has refused to handle James' body because he has AIDS. People have already started talking. This is a small town and the talking will never stop. People in this town liked James. He was a caring person, kind to his mother. He didn't deserve this.

"I don't think you set the fire, Neary, but I'm dead certain that you gave the virus to James. I can't lay a murder charge but I can lay a mischief charge, or just have the story leaked to the newspaper. My patience with you, Neary, is wearing thin."

"This is blackmail... you can't do that."

"Try me."

"So that's how it goes," said Neary, wearily. "You want me to get out... leave."

"You got me right. You're a selfish bastard, church organist or not, and poor James paid the price."

David left his office with a great deal of satisfaction. That's one bad apple taken care of

Chapter 29

"Did you bring me back a fresh cuppa?" yelled Clancy from the inner office. "You forgot! You forgot! You lazy swine. What am I going to do with you? David, my boy, you need a good kick in the butt. I'm tired of holding the fort while you meander around, over hill and dale, and I sit here caffeine starved."

"Is Greg not around?"

"Greg is out on a call. Some teenagers broke into a cottage and he's gone to find out if he can get some nice fingerprints or tire tracks."

"Was much stolen?"

"Nothing much of value. Window broken that sort of thing."

The phone rang. "Wonder who that can be?" Clancy picked up the phone then, held it out to David. "This one's for you, David, sounds like a nice lady on the phone and boy has she got the hots for you, all panting, deep breathing and the like...."

David was in no mood for games. "Yes," he replied crisply.

"Constable Scott, I believe I have some information that would be helpful to you regarding Cathy Snifton." It was the halting but shrill voice of old Miss Temple. Did she think he was deaf?

"Proceed."

"I just remembered something. The evening that Miss Snifton was murdered, I was out to get a little fresh air and to get some exercise before I retired. I need to exercise in order to sleep at night, otherwise I toss and turn worrying about my problems, like who is going to look after my cats after I'm gone. Who is going to feed them? Who is going to love them? I decided to walk along the perimeter of the park. It's well-lit at that time of night."

"Get to the point, please."

"As I was walking along, I saw Cathy in a car at the parking lot with a man. I wasn't going along looking into parked cars.

I was just walking through the park minding my own business. The man she was with rolled down the window and shouted at me. Dear me, such language, I hesitate to repeat it."

"What did he say? What were his exact words?"

"First of all he said, 'Fuck off, you nosey old broad.' Then he accelerated his car directly at me, almost ran me down, almost killed me. I thought I was going to have a heart attack. Thank heavens I was able to step aside in time."

"What time was this?"

"It was around ten p.m."

"What was the make of the car?"

"It was a blue Ford."

Mm, thought David.

"Did you recognize the man?"

"No, but if I saw him again, I certainly would. He was in his early forties, black hair, round face with a small scar under his right eyebrow. He was wearing a black parka."

"Are you sure it was Cathy? Why didn't you tell me about this?"

"That evening, the shock of it had been so unpleasant that I'd blotted it out of my mind."

"I wish you had told me sooner," said David, "but the information has been very helpful. Thank you."

"Well," said David, smiling at Clancy, "I got a hot tip from a hot old lady. See you later."

Her description of a forty-year-old man with a scar under his right eyebrow fits Ted Chirp to a T. Not to mention his foul language and angry outburst. Ted Chirp is a man I want to talk to real soon.

*****

David was trying to straighten up the mess on his desk before sitting down to concentrate on the information that he'd just received. He dumped some of the empty Tim Horton's coffee cups into the waste paper basket. Then he overheard Clancy in the front office say, "You'll find him back there among the coffee cups."

Into the room walked a very unhappy Gale Chirp. He

remembered her sitting in the front row with the rest of the church choir at Cathy Snifton's funeral. Her eyes were bloodshot and a tear trickled down her cheek.

With trembling hands, she held out to him a piece of paper. "I received this under my door this morning. Here, read it."

David unfolded the piece of paper on which had been crudely pasted large letters, probably taken from a newspaper headline: same paper texture. No one types threatening notes anymore. They glue them together from cut out letters.

The note read, *'Death to the Fornicators'*. David suppressed a smile, 'fornicators', what an old fashioned biblical expression, hardly current coin.

"Mr. Scott, I'm a single woman now, living alone with two children." She looked down at her hands, "My husband and I have separated. We live apart. I'm taking this note very seriously. I've brought it to you and I want you to do something. We have a murderer loose in our community and he hasn't been caught."

David studied the note again. Was the threat real, or was it a prank? Or the product of a sick mind?

"Do you know of anyone who might, or would write this note? Someone who wants to scare you, maybe intimidate you? David paused and gave Gale a hard look, "Your husband? He's the first one that I can think of. He has beaten you in the past. He strikes me as the kind of guy who would write a poison pen note. Do you think he wrote it?

"No, no, no. It's not his style. He's more physical and direct. He wouldn't act in a sneaky way by slipping a note under my door."

"Do you know for certain? When was the last time you saw him? Did he mention anything about reconciliation? He might be using this tactic to get back with you, figuring that you would need his protection and help. He tried to hurt you in the past."

Gale reflected for a moment. "Usually he acted out of anger and frustration when he'd been drinking. It's the drinking that's done it to him. The last time we met, he told me that he was going to join A.A."

"Who else would put it there?"

"I have no idea."

David tried a new tack, "Have you seen any strangers hanging around your place, phoney repairmen coming to your door, cable TV installers that you haven't called? Have you seen anyone parked across the street for a long time, or down the street watching the house?"

"No, not that I have noticed."

"My best advice is to keep your blinds closed. When you're on the street be aware of people behind you and keep alert. Have you had any strange phone calls?"

"None."

"This might be a one-time occurrence. See if it escalates."

"I might be dead by then."

"The note refers to more than one person. Can you think of another adult that the writer might be referring to, other than your husband?"

"Can't think of anyone."

"Well, I'll drive by your house several times in the evenings and see if everything is okay, beginning with this evening."

"That would be reassuring. Thank you."

"In the meantime, call me if anything else happens."

Gale picked up her purse and left. 'Fornicate' is such an old fashioned word thought David. Why not adulterers? It goes back to the Old Testament. Strange. It's the kind of language that Miss Temple might use. But she's too scared herself at the moment to be running around Mariposa uttering death threats, unless she's gone completely barmy. Maybe I should pay her another visit.

She's the only one so far that is obsessed with the Bible He knocked on the door of her cottage. A very pale Miss Temple peered through the letter slot, then opened the door. Dressed all in black, she appeared very downcast.

"May I come in?"

"Yes, certainly, if you must. I'm in mourning."

"In mourning?"

"Yes, for my dead cat."

"Any idea yet who did it?"

"None."

"I didn't come to see you about your cat. I came to ask you about death threats. Have you been getting any more?"

"No, I just got the one."

"And you have no idea who sent it?"

"It could be anyone."

"Does the word, 'fornicators', mean anything to you?" He stared hard at her to see if her face would give her away. But Miss Temple didn't blush or look flustered. There was no change in her demeanor. Miss Temple thought for a moment then said, "It's an Old Testament expression for those who commit adultery or have relationships outside of marriage. Is that any help at all to you? A good Oxford dictionary should help. Why do you want to know? Why are you asking?"

"No particular reason. If you see anything unusual or receive another death threat, give me a call. Have the phone calls continued?"

"No, they seem to have stopped."

"Let's keep in touch, Miss Temple. If you feel threatened in any way, call." With that David got up and left. From the way she'd answered his last question, she didn't send the note.

Why focus on this? This was a small problem. He now had three murder cases to solve, Cathy Snifton and James Muir and his mother.

Chapter 30

He knew the rock he could find Ted Chirp under, so he headed for his real estate office, Real Deal. Ted was alone in the back of the room, shuffling papers and putting his desk in order. David plunked himself down right in front of the desk

"I'm surprised to see you again. What brings you here? I thought I answered all of your questions," said Ted

"Not all. I have some more for you. You say that the last time you saw Cathy Snifton was several weeks ago? You lied."

"Who is telling you different?"

"You saw her Friday night didn't you, even though she didn't come to Happy Hour at Brewery Bay. You met up with her later."

"Now don't go jumping to conclusions. Yes, alright, I did meet up with her."

"What time were you there?"

"Around ten p.m."

"Did you see anyone in the park that you recognized?"

"No one."

"Are you sure? We have a witness who places you in the park at that time. Apparently, according to my witness, you tried to run her down with your car."

"Geez, that old bitch ratted on me."

"I could charge you with assault and battery, but since she is not pressing charges, I won't, if you co-operate. What did Cathy want from you?"

"She told me she was pregnant, but I swear I wasn't the father. She wanted money. I gave her what I had and said I would give her more on Monday when the banks opened."

"Why did you give her money, if you weren't the father? What would be the point?"

"The point is that she might tell my wife that I was having an affair with her and then I would be sunk. She could say anything and I would be up the creek, don't you see? I wasn't in a position to say 'no' to her request."

"That's a good motive for murder. Blackmail."

166

"For a couple of hundred dollars would I murder someone? You must be joking. You can't pin that on me."

"Try me. Most blackmailers aren't satisfied. They keep coming back for more and more. It might never end."

"I swear that I had nothing to do with her murder. She and I had an understanding."

"What did she do after that?"

"She claimed she wanted to walk home. She got out of the car and I drove home."

"Why did she stay in the park?"

"I don't know, but that is how it happened although I don't expect you to believe me.

"I went back to my place, a rental arrangement that I have temporarily until I get back with my wife."

"And you never saw her after that? You never saw her leave the park?"

"I respected her wishes. She wanted to walk home. Just like I told you, she got out of the car and I drove home."

"Just like that "

"That's how it happened. That's the truth."

"Was Cathy staying in the park to meet someone, do you think?"

"She just said, let me out, I'll walk home."

"Be on standby, Ted. I'll need you for further questioning. You were the last person to see Cathy alive."

Chapter 31

The heat in the office was oppressive. The radiator was hissing and clanking like a steam engine. We need a humidifier in here, thought David, standing at the window, but who's going to pay for it? With his hand he wiped a spot on the glass. The windows needed to be washed too. But spring cleaning was a bloody long way off. Outside, the snow was pelting down, another grim day.

As he walked back to his desk, he noticed Reverend Day standing quietly in the doorway. David wasn't surprised to see him. He'd figured that the blue Toyota was his. He was kind of expecting Day to show up eventually. He had a lot of explaining to do.

David waited while Day reached up to loosen his wool scarf and stuff it into his track jacket.

"Take a seat. Would you like a cup of coffee?"

"No thanks."

"You were the man in the park, week after week, sitting in your car watching Cathy whirl around the ice, weren't you?"

David waited for the answer. The only sounds in the room now were coming from the outer office, from the police radio.

Reverend Day coughed and then uncrossed his legs.

"Yes, yes it was me. Confession is good for the soul. Yes, I was involved with Cathy. I loved her. I've denied this until now, because of shame, my deep shame. I had hoped that the whole situation would just vanish, disappear, but it hasn't.

"I hope in telling you that this guilt, which has laid so heavily on my shoulders, will be lifted. I want to make a clean breast of the situation to you. It's not easy. When this comes out at the meeting of the Board of Stewards down at the church, I will become just another middle-aged man with no job and no prospects. I'm curious to know how you tied me in with Cathy? How did you discover that I'd been involved with her?"

"Someone recognized your car down at the park and

168

noticed that it was often parked there. The sticker on your license plate, which was recently removed, is fairly recognizable, *Honk if you love Jesus.*"

"Truth will always out," sighed Billy. "Yes, I was the one who used to sit in my car looking out at the lake and the skating rink. I'd park my car and watch the skaters. I loved the flash of colour, their red mitts and scarves, their flushed cheeks, their youthfulness, their joy at being outdoors. I guess I wanted to capture some of that feeling. How elusive those emotions are!" Day ran his fingers along the zipper on his jacket.

"How did you get involved with her?" asked David softly.

"It all started out so innocently. When I was working late on my sermon, in my study down at the church, I used to come out and find Cathy sitting on the bench after choir practice, reading a book. She would stop reading and ask me some questions. I found her pleasant. There were many young, attractive women in the choir and in the congregation," said Day. "Every minister is surrounded by women, more so than men. But what attracted me to her was her cheerful disposition."

A sitting duck, thought David.

"Because it was late at night, I would offer her a lift home. Cathy told me how unhappy she was in this small town, how tied she was to her mother who suffered from severe arthritis. She felt so ashamed of her home. She could never bring anyone there. Her mother was a television zombie. Cathy wanted to get away. She hated her job and her home life was not much better."

"I told her that no-one's life is without its share of problems. It's how we deal with them, how we come to terms with them. I counselled her that we must be patient, we must try to make it better with God's help and prayer."

Prayer obviously wasn't enough, thought David with a wry smile. People can get into a lot of trouble on their knees.

"Before she got out of the car, Cathy would give me a hug, a way of thanking me for the ride.

"About once a week I would find her on my way out of

my office and I would offer her a ride home, out of kindness, out of concern. Several weeks after this started, we were talking in my car. I had driven her down to the lake, because she said that she wanted to see the sky at dusk. It was a beautiful evening—the last warm days of Indian summer. The colour of the leaves was changing. There was a golden lushness to everything. Cathy was sitting very close to me. I could smell her body. I could feel her heat. She leaned closer to me, to pick a hair off my collar. One thing led to another. I tried to stop her, but I was putty in her skilful little hands. I was weak as water."

David noticed that beads of sweat had broken out on Day's brow.

"It was over before I knew what had happened. I was so ashamed. I blamed myself. I prayed to God for forgiveness. I asked Cathy for forgiveness. I wanted to be struck down by lightning or to drop dead in the street. But nothing happened.

"I should have realised how weak I was. How vulnerable I was. I avoided Cathy successfully for a week. I worked on my sermons at home. Mabel must have thought this was strange, but she never asked me why. She never confronted me. She never challenged me. She just accepted everything blindly. She never noticed my anguish, my struggle to avoid sin. Had Mabel confronted me it might have prevented what was to follow."

Reverend Day held his head in his hands. "Do you realize how desperately I struggled? I avoided Cathy but it was hard to keep from bumping into her. No matter where I was, I would bump in to her. I was fighting against forces that were pulling me under. Then the inevitable would happen again and afterwards I would swear that was the last time."

David shook his head. All this breast beating. Not getting enough at home and opportunity knocks.

"I honestly thought it would never happen again."

"Really?" said David, while silently thinking, how naive.

Day looked down at his running shoes. "I lied to myself. I was a married man. What right did I have to be in her life? I'd sit in the park watching her skate. If she had a date, with someone after skating then I would just go home on my own. But if no one picked her up, she would simply come over and ask for a lift and I would drop her off."

"You were the one who gave her the music box with the skater on the top."

"Yes. It was a sentimental gesture on my part. I couldn't give her anything else. I couldn't take her out on a date, so when I saw the music box with the skater on it, I bought it for her."

"Were you there on Friday nights?"

"Not usually. I knew on Friday Cathy was busy with her other friends. I didn't want to interfere."

"What about Friday, December, the thirteenth, the night she was murdered?"

"I phoned her that afternoon to see how she was"

"What time?"

"Three-thirty."

David had figured that the cultured voice on the phone was Day's.

"Where did you call from?"

"The house. We have a phone in the living room and an extension up in the bedroom for emergencies—people call from the hospital when someone is dying, a relative phones and asks me to come right over. I told Mabel that I was going upstairs after lunch to have a nap. I made the call from my bedroom. She told me that she was in some kind of trouble. 'What kind of trouble?' I asked. 'Are you pregnant? Just say yes, or no'. She answered 'Yes'. I trusted that she was taking care of things. I had left everything up to her. I asked her what she wanted me to do? If she wanted me to come right down that evening. She said that she would meet me later in the park, near the skating rink around ten-thirty. I promised to come. I promised to do everything in my power. I got off the phone in a daze and tried to collect my thoughts. I was elated that I was going to be a father. I felt joyful. I wanted to the right thing for Cathy and for the child, my child.

"My head said the situation was impossible. Cathy and I had so little in common. That's what my head said, but my heart said, I want Cathy and I want the child. I was willing to

171

give up everything, my job, this town, everything for the sake of this child. The heart has its reasons.

"Going downstairs, I told Mabel that an emergency had arisen and that I had to attend to it."

"Did Mabel suspect anything?"

"No," said Day sharply," she never suspects anything. I went out for a bite to eat to cool my head off and decide what to do. After putting in a few hours, I went down to the park as we had arranged over the phone. There was so much for us to discuss. It was hard to wait until ten-thirty. It was the longest evening in my life. I couldn't go to the bar, not someone in my position. She wasn't there on time. I got out of my car and began looking for her. I finally found her. I recognized her from a distance by her red mohair scarf and mittens. She was arguing loudly with a man. They were arguing so loudly, she hadn't heard my approach. Suddenly, she slapped his face. Then he pushed her down in the snow. Getting up she lunged at him. I had to protect her before she got seriously hurt."

"Did you get a chance to get a good look at him?"

Day was evasive. "His back was to me. All my attention was focused on Cathy. I had to protect her before she got seriously hurt."

"What time was this?"

"Around eleven p.m."

"My main concern was to protect Cathy, but she wanted none of it. Instead, she angrily shouted at me to mind my own business. To go wait in the car. 'Butt out, buddy,' said her companion. They then took off along the shore to continue their argument. I watched them leave and then decided to follow them. I was very worried about what he might do to Cathy. The snow was really deep and they weren't sticking to the path. When I finally caught up to them again, they were still yelling at each other. I heard Cathy say, 'You owe me', to which he replied, 'Ooh, yeah.'"

"Did you get a good look at him? Would you recognize him again?"

"Yes."

"Continue."

I lunged at him, grabbing his arm. Cathy yelled at me.

I heard him say, "The lady said, stay out of this. Who are you to butt in?" The last thing I heard was Cathy screaming, 'Don't.'

"The next thing I knew was that I was flat on my face in the snow with Cathy standing over me. My nose was bleeding. I could hardly see. Cathy helped me to a bench and she said she would go and get help."

"What happened to your assailant?"

"He disappeared after he slugged me. I don't know where he went. I was sitting in a daze on the park bench. Cathy said that she would call my wife and ask her to come and get me. She was going to make up some story and use a different name. She went off to make the phone call at the pay phone near the skating rink. That was the last time I saw her alive," said Day bitterly.

"This is very important. Do you have any idea of where Cathy went after the time she left you to go make a phone call?"

"None. She just said, she was going to phone for help."

"Reverend Day, you knew who decked you. It was Ted Chirp."

"I never mentioned his name."

"But it was him, wasn't it?"

"Yes," Day whispered, "It was him."

"You think he killed Cathy?"

"I don't know. I don't know. How can I point a finger at anyone? Let him without sin cast the first stone. I let Cathy be murdered. Instead of protecting her, I let this happen. Can't you see how badly I felt? And the worst thing was that afterwards I couldn't remember a thing. I had completely blotted out what had happened that evening in my mind. It must have been shock. The next day I woke up with a lump on the back of my head and I couldn't remember how I got it. No one will ever know the personal grief this has caused me."

"Did Cathy indicate in any way that she might not come back?"

"No, nothing. I watched her hurrying in the direction of the phone booth. I believed her and I waited. That was the last I saw of her."

"Weren't you worried that something must have happened when she didn't come back?"

"I wasn't thinking properly. I was just out of it. I relied on Cathy to get help. I was in no position to get up and phone myself. I just sat there.

"I waited and waited. I thought that Cathy hadn't been able to get hold of Mabel she was probably sound asleep and hadn't heard the phone. I waited half an hour."

"Do you think that Cathy ever made that phone call? Do you think she ever got to that phone booth?"

"I don't know. I just don't know."

"I waited and waited. At least forty-five minutes. Tom Ball came by with his dog. Actually his dog found me. He'd let him off his leash for a good run and he came tearing through the bushes, skidded in front of the bench and began barking. Tom must have thought that I was drunk. I was mortified. I told him that I'd fallen. He didn't ask any questions. He just helped me walk through the park. I made it home."

"Do you have any idea of where Chirp went after he hit you?"

"No."

"When you got home, did you notice the time?"

"Just that it was after midnight."

"Was Mabel up? Did you talk to her about what had happened?"

"How could I? I couldn't bring myself to tell Mabel anything. I hoped that the whole thing was just a dream that it would blow over. My head was throbbing and I just stumbled upstairs to bed."

"When did you learn about her death?"

"The next day. I knew instinctively that somehow I was involved. But how? What did I know? I went over and over again trying to recall what had happened that night. Bit by bit my memory came back. My doctor said that I'd suffered a concussion when I fell down."

"Do you think you murdered her? If Cathy were dead, it would let you out of an extremely embarrassing situation."

"Do you think that I would go that far? Commit murder?"

David shrugged. "Someone did. And she wasn't black-mailing you? You had a lot to lose. Your job, your marriage."

"Cathy was a dear, sweet girl. You've got her all wrong." Day gave him a hot, angry glare.

"You've heard the old maxim; you've got to be cruel to be kind. You might as well know now rather than later, Cathy was sexually involved with three men, as far as I can make out, including you, on and off over a considerable period of time. I doubt if she really knew who the father was. All Cathy knew was that she was in a jam and she needed help. Whom could she lean on?"

Day's face turned pale. "That's a lie. I can't believe it. It's not true. She wasn't like that."

"It's true," said David, softly. He waited. He could hear the hissing of the radiator, the windows rattling and even Day's own laboured breathing. Outside in the hall, he could hear Clancy chatting happily away to a young girl who had lost her purse.

"May I have drink of water?"

"Sure." David went over to the water cooler and filled a paper cup from the dispenser.

"Thanks."

Day took a few sips of water. "I'm going home now. I feel a little under the weather."

David nodded. "I'll have your statement typed up. Drop around tomorrow and I'll have you sign it."

"Certainly."

Day slumped out of the office, a world-weary man.

David watched him go. There goes a very depressed man, wiser but a great deal sadder.

Chapter 32

There was some checking to do. The phone calls made from the booth in the park. Did Cathy phone the Day residence? He contacted Bell Canada for the number of calls made from that booth on Friday, the thirteenth, the time, and the length of time they took. It took two days for them to get back to him with the information. He looked down at the computer print-out. Yes, there was a call to the Day residence at eleven-thirty p.m. from the booth in the park.

He phoned the Day residence. Mabel Day came on the line. "Mabel, did you receive a phone call on the night of Friday, December thirteenth, near midnight? It's very important to this case. Can you remember?"

"That would be way past my bedtime. Offhand I can't recall. My memory is not good."

"The phone call lasted three minutes. It would have been from a young woman."

"We get so many calls, some emergencies. It's hard to sort out one from another."

"I see," said David. "I'll be dropping in on Reverend Day this evening to have him sign something. I would like you to be present to help me further in my inquiries."

"I don't see how I can be much more helpful."

"Think about the phone call and I'll ask you again this evening."

Three minutes. How could she forget a three-minute phone call?

Chapter 33

At 7 p.m. David rang the bell. Reverend Day, in sweat pants and slippers and holding the evening newspaper, met him at the front door.

"Come in and sit down and make yourself comfortable." Day indicated a comfortable but worn sofa chair in the living room off the front hall.

"I've brought your statement and want you to sign it." David pulled out the document from his briefcase. "Is Mabel in? It's important that I talk to her also."

"Yes by all means. She's around here somewhere. We had an early supper. At the table, she said that she had another one of her migraine headaches. She went upstairs to lie down. I'll call her." Day went over to the bottom of the stairs.

"Mabel," he yelled, "Dave Scott, from the OPP is here to see you."

They listened in silence.

"Mm, that's funny. Maybe she dozed off. Excuse me a minute while I go and wake her up."

David watched him bound up the stairs and then move along to the end of the hall. He heard him pause at the bedroom and give a light tap on the door before opening it. Day called back to him. "She's not in the bedroom lying down. She's probably in the bathroom having a good soak."

Day knocked on the bathroom door. "Mabel, Mabel, are you in there? Dave Scott of the OPP needs your help. Shall I tell him that you will be down in a few minutes?"

Again no answer. Day tried the door handle. "That's funny, it's locked." He rattled the door handle. "Mabel, it's me." Then he noticed some water seeping out from under the door. He pounded and shouted, "Mabel, are you in there?"

He shouted down to David, "Something's wrong. I'm sure she's in there. I can hear the tap running. She might have had a stroke. We've got to break down the door."

David bounded up the stairs, two steps at a time. "Stand back and let me take care of it." He took a run at the door and it gave way with a mighty crash. Inside, the sight chilled his blood.

Through the steam clouded room, he spied Mabel staring at him with dull eyes, sitting upright in the overflowing tub, with a slashed wrist hanging over the side. Blood was everywhere.

"Oh my God. Oh no," whispered Day.

"Call an ambulance. I'll put tourniquets on." David tore a face towel from the hand rail and ripped it into strips. Once he got her wrists bound, he pulled her heavy body out of the tub and laid her carefully down on the white tiled floor, which was a sea of blood and water. He began cardiac massage in an effort to get a pulse.

Why was the ambulance taking so long?

A small voice within David said, "No matter what you do, no matter how hard you try, you can't save her. You're too late."

He heard the ambulance siren and running feet on the stairs. A doctor knelt down by Mabel, felt the pulse in her neck and then took out a hypodermic needle, filled it and jabbed it into her heart.

They waited.

But it was no use, Mabel Day was no longer in this world.

David followed the stretcher down the stairs. In the darkened living room, he found Day sitting in a chair, in a daze.

"Please, please, don't go yet. I... I desperately need your help," said Day, reaching out his hand towards David. "I need to understand. I can't understand any of this. I want to know why. Why? My God, why? Why would she do such a crazy thing? She had everything to live for? Why? Why would she kill herself? She never told me that she was unhappy."

"Didn't she?" said David softly.

"She never told me that she was. Why do you say that?"

"The reason I came over this evening was to question Mabel about the phone call that Cathy made to your home that evening that she was murdered. She did go for help for you that evening. She did make that call.

"I talked to Mabel a couple of days ago from my office. Mabel told me that she never got that call, that she was sound asleep. What motive had she to lie?

"Bell Canada Records say that Cathy made the call which

lasted several minutes. She was murdered about forty-five minutes after she made that call in the park by someone who knew that she'd be there."

"Oh, no! What you're saying is that Cathy talked to Mabel and Mabel figured out who was making the call."

"You guess right."

"I was never unkind to Mabel. I kept my relationship with Cathy a secret. I never discussed my relationship or my feelings about her. In our conversation Mabel gave no hint, no reproach, no anger. I thought everything was alright."

"But she did know," said David. "Didn't you notice any signs that she was coming apart at the seams?"

Day reflected for a few moments, then said, "Looking back, I did notice that she had been complaining about not getting enough sleep. But I thought that would pass. A lot of people complain about not getting enough sleep. And there were other things. But I put it down to the change of life. Mabel was never a happy person. But to commit murder. I can't believe a woman that I've been married to for, it must be twenty-two years, would do this. It's impossible to believe...her of all people."

"All of us are capable. It's just that inhibitions keep our impulses under control. Mabel knew. She listened in on your phone conversations. She didn't want to admit to you or herself that you were cheating on her. But the anger was there. She had no outlet for expressing her anger at you for deceiving her. It just kept building. When she listened in on your conversation with Cathy and found out she was pregnant, it blew her mind. She had to do something or she would lose everything. But what? Then Cathy's phone call came that night saying that you were hurt. Why did you stay with Mabel if things weren't going well?"

"I felt I had to. I felt I owed it to her."

David gave a wry smile. "Divorce is better than murder. There were plenty of signs and you didn't pick up on them. Mabel did it in the heat of the moment. She murdered Cathy because she feared that she would lose everything."

Day slumped in his chair. "It's all so awful and I thought she knew nothing when she knew everything."

David went to the front door and quietly let himself out.

179

*****

Next morning, when David arrived early at the office, Clancy was bouncing around the room, like a bumblebee that had just discovered a motherlode of honey. He could hardly suppress his curiosity. David on the other hand felt no joy, just emotionally drained. He would have preferred a much different ending than the suicide of Mabel Day.

"Hey, pal, come on," squealed Clancy like a kid expecting candy, "spill the beans. You owe me one. Stop holding out on me. You've solved the Snifton murder case. Am I right? I heard about Mabel Day's suicide on the radio this morning. I want to hear every detail. Don't leave a thing out." Clancy gave him a playful slap on the buns.

"Clancy, don't get your balls in an uproar. Let me get my report written up and then I'll be with you." David sat down at his computer and began typing. Clancy came over to his desk and peered over his shoulder.

"Oh hell, Clancy, you're making me nervous. I'll fill you in.

"Apparently, Mabel Day hadn't been sleeping for months. She had been lying awake wondering where her husband was. He said that he was at prayer meetings."

"At prayer meetings?" laughed Clancy, "That's a new excuse."

"She wanted to believe for a long time that her husband was where he said he was. She desperately wanted to trust him, but ugly rumours started to surface, about his car being parked late at night down by the lake or in front of the Chirp house. She didn't know what to think. She was worried. She didn't confront him but she watched and waited. When Billy made phone calls up in their bedroom, she would listen on the downstairs extension. As the affair with Cathy progressed, she became more and more alarmed. When Day phoned Cathy at the library that afternoon, and she found out that Cathy was pregnant, she assumed that Billy was the father.

"It must have been Mabel who phoned the library and threatened Cathy. She was the one to whom Miss Lemon

180

overheard Cathy saying, "It's none of your business. Stay out of my life, but later in the evening when Cathy called from the pay phone in the park, Mabel recognized her voice. She rushed down to the park to have it out with Cathy. She met up with her and suggested that they have a frank talk down by the lake, out of sight and away from everyone. Cathy probably told her everything. From Mabel's point of view, this arrogant bitch wanted to destroy her husband's career, his reputation and their marriage. There would be nothing left.

"In a flash, she reached out and grabbed the ends of Cathy's scarf and pulled. I don't think Mabel had a plan. It just happened. Mabel, a tall, strong woman had great reserves of energy, all that pent up anger simmering for so many months with no outlet.

"Taken by surprise, Cathy was no match for her. Cathy might have had a chance if she'd had some warning, but she didn't. It took only a few short minutes to snuff out Cathy's life

"Mabel was very lucky. No one had seen her. No one knew that she had come to the park. After she'd finished strangling Cathy, she was lucky again. She saw Billy's car in the parking lot and drove home. Billy was still in the park and he was injured. When she got back to the house, she went quickly upstairs and pretended to be asleep. Tom Ball helped Billy home. When Billy stumbled into the house, he was in such a daze that he didn't notice anything. He just took off his shoes and climbed into bed. What helped her further was that the next morning, Day couldn't recall a thing about the previous evening. He had emotional amnesia."

"Now, isn't that something!"

"Intuitively, Day knew that he was connected with the park that evening in some way. But he didn't know how. Imagine his shock when he heard that Cathy had been murdered. This amnesia persisted for some time, but bits and pieces eventually started to bubble to the surface.

"Mabel, on the other hand, thought that with Cathy out of the way everything would be fine, things would return to normal. The threat to their marriage was over. She had saved Billy from disaster. But things became dicey when I was questioning Billy. I was getting too close. Mabel wanted suspicion directed away from her husband. She wanted a scapegoat, a fall guy.

"When she heard James talking to Billy in the living room saying how guilty he felt and how depressed he was and that he wished he could have saved Cathy if only he had stayed longer in the park, Mabel wasn't sure whether James, on the off chance, might have seen something. But he hadn't.

"James was the perfect fall guy, depressed, sick and suffering misplaced guilt. He was the perfect victim. James, in the town's eyes, was Cathy's boyfriend. Everyone could be persuaded that he did it.

"Despite what most people thought, including Mabel, James deeply cared for Cathy. He had no motive for killing her. He was not the father of her unborn child and they were on good terms as friends. James felt guilty because he cared for Cathy and also because he was in the park the same evening that she was killed, having sex with Neary.

"After James left their house, Mabel hatched her plan. The next night, she took a can of kerosene and doused the back of the Muir house. Torching the wooden frame house was easy, it went up like a tinderbox. James and his mother were upstairs.

"When I met Mabel standing on the front lawn, she was shaking, not from the cold, but from fear. She was worried that the firemen might save James and get him out alive. She tried to point the finger of guilt at James that night. I just put it down to anxiety and worry. He had been suicidal she said. I dismissed her ideas as mere figments of her imagination. Mabel watched the fire knowing that she had set it. She stayed on the lawn of the house until both Mrs. Muir and James' body were pulled out. When James died in the hospital, case closed, she figured. Suspicion for Cathy's murder would be removed from her husband. Day would be safe."

"Hey, isn't that the limit," said Clancy.

"But to Mabel's dismay, she began noticing once again that Billy wasn't coming home right after prayer meetings. Miss Temple and others were making hints about Gale Chirp. Mabel sent a death note to Gale to see what would happen, to scare her off. I believe eventually she would have done away with Gale."

"It never stops with one murder, does it?" said Clancy fingering a paperclip.

"She figured it was all over when I phoned Day saying that I wanted to talk to her. So she slashed her wrists. Either way she had nothing to live for."

"Ain't that something else," exclaimed Clancy. "I'd figured that it would be Ted Chirp, because of his violent history."

"You and me. For a long time I thought so. But Chirp, after he socked Day on the chops, immediately high-tailed it. Oh, by the way, he's the guy that was mooning on Miss Temple's lawn and probably strangled her cat. I can't prove this, so it's mere speculation on my part."

"How is Day taking it?"

"He's bewildered by it all. Until this, the whole scandal of his involvement with Cathy Snifton would be a thing of the painful past. He's lucky, because if Mabel had lived to go on trial, he would be out of a job and out of the town. He'd never be able to live it down. Day is a scared man. Life goes on," said David, "and I've got to write up this report!"

After Clancy had heard enough to be satisfied and was asking no more questions, David concentrated on his report. He glanced up to see Mildred Lemon standing in the doorway. She was wearing a bright green winter coat with a matching scarf. He was surprised to see her again. She'd changed. She had stopped slumping. She was standing straight and tall. Her face was fuller. She had a touch of powder on her nose and a dash of red on her lips. She no longer looked thin and miserable. That humble, hang-dog expression had gone.

"I've come to tell you," she said, "that I appreciate all your efforts in catching Cathy's killer. I assume that the suicide of Mabel Day indicated that she had killed Cathy. Who would have believed that Mrs. Day could have done this terrible thing to my friend? She must have been crazy."

"Quite," echoed David.

"I want you to know that it's all helped me to make up my mind. I can't bring Cathy back. I asked myself, do I want to continue feeling lonely, empty and miserable, or do I want to do something about it? I've handed in my notice to Mrs. Proudfoot."

"That takes courage, Mildred. How did she take it?"

"At first she just accepted it. Then she began wheedling, like a weasel, offering me all kinds of bribes, hoping that I would change my mind. She was oh so nice, so awfully nice, all smiles and soooo polite. There was no more of, 'Do this, Mildred, and after you've finished doing that, do this'. Right away I had a proper coffee break in the morning, and a tea break in the afternoon, something that I didn't use to get. She advertised my job for several weeks in the Mariposa Packet, but all she got were high school dropouts who couldn't have cared less about working there. The library to them was in the same category as working at MacDonald's. She asked me to reconsider. The pay is terrible at the Library, barely minimum wage. Mrs. Proudfoot should have realized long ago, good help is hard to find."

"What will you do, Mildred?"

"I've been thinking of working with young people. I like their enthusiasm, energy and freshness."

David watched Mildred leave his office with a determined step. Blessed are the meek for they shall inherit the earth, flashed through his mind. Now where had he heard that phrase before?

*****

The first robin, the first sign of spring, flew to a branch on the tree outside his bedroom window. David's spirits immediately lifted. It had been a long, tough winter, with blizzards, white-outs and storms. Now the good weather would soon be here. He had something to look forward to. Saturday morning, the sun was shining, and all was right with the world. David had a strong urge to be amongst people. No, not everyone. He wanted to be with Clara. Where would she be this morning? Probably shopping down at the outdoor market, looking at the pussy willows, yellow forsythia, pots of crocuses and daffodils. That's what women do on a lovely spring Saturday morning, shop. He'd go and do the same, buy some cheese, and vegetables and some fresh Macintosh apples for his empty refrigerator. At the same time, he'd walk around and take in the scene. Even if he didn't run into her, at least he'd let the townspeople know he was amongst the living.

He passed the stalls of fresh, Mennonite sausage, with chains of sausage hanging on hooks. A Mennonite farm woman, her hair tied back with a kerchief, extended a fork to him, so he could lift off the small bit of hot sausage. Delicious. He bought a kilogram. Next, he passed the tables of fresh organic herbs, parsley, thyme, basil, oregano. Great for salads and for rabbits.

He gave a brief glance at the home-made crocheted pot holders, the embroidered dish cloths, tea towels, and pillow slips. He wasn't ready for that yet.

He looked over the boxes of red potatoes and hot-house tomatoes, squash, and turnip, and bought some.

He passed the health stall where a woman was stuffing raw carrots into a juicer. It takes a lot of carrots for a glass of carrot juice, thought David. The things that people do to get healthy. He shook his head. Next on his list was some old cheddar cheese, which was nice to sprinkle on hot chilli, and some cheese curds for snacks.

Then, something caused him to look up momentarily from the tables, a flash of light. Far across the parking lot full of tables and people, he spied a blond head amongst the browns and the grey bending over to examine an arrangement of dried flowers. David moved closer to make sure. It must be her. She lifted her head. Those big, brown eyes stared straight at him and then quickly lowered.

David pushed quickly through the crowd, past shopping carts, dogs on leashes, babies in strollers, past the baskets and chairs, to where Clara was standing.

"Can I buy you a mug of hot cider to keep off the chill?" asked David, wondering how she'd react to his suggestion.

"That would be nice," said Clara, blushing.

David smiled, "At least we are on speaking terms. That's a good sign."

"Barely," replied Clara, but she returned his smile.

"It's not nice to bear grudges against your fellow man. If I have hurt your feelings, I want to apologize," David said.

"I didn't think the police apologized about anything. It's not in keeping with their macho image."

"Not true. Contrary to what you may think, I'm very soft hearted."

Clara smiled. "I've a confession, too. I've always hated you because you were always trying to tell me that Tom was a shit. I didn't believe you and I resented you trying to prove it to me. I didn't want to believe it. I guess love was blind. I was too blind to see that he wasn't interested in me and that he would never have made me happy."

"We all make mistakes in judgement, Clara. I make mistakes, too. It just shows that we're both human."

"I refused to accept what I saw. I refused to let go. You were only doing your job."

"Clara, let's begin again. Let's start fresh, right here and now. Finish your shopping. I'll give you a ride home, take your groceries in, and then we'll go for a spin in the country. We'll have lunch at the Old Mill Inn. They make delicious corn bread. It's home-style cooking."

"That's one offer, I can't say 'no' to. Will you come with me, while I pick up a few more things and then we'll go?"

"Clara, that'll be no problem. I've got all the time in the world."